Return of the Traveller

by the same author

THE WILD GOOSE CHASE
THE AERODROME
THE PROFESSOR
POEMS

RETURN OF THE TRAVELLER

REX WARNER

J. B. LIPPINCOTT COMPANY
PHILADELPHIA   NEW YORK

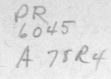
*Published in Great Britain
under the title
"Why Was I Killed?"*

To Basil Wright

CONTENTS

Return of the Traveller

Prologue

...I CONTINUALLY wonder how I may account for my present state, which, I suppose, it would be accurate to describe as one of death. To normal persons and scenes I can approach closely enough; indeed, my vision and hearing seem alike preternaturally clear. Yet something cuts me off utterly from the sights and acquaintances of my life even in the moment when I am revisiting them in a bright light and with the greatest enthusiasm. The questions that I ask are unheard or go unheeded, nor can I pick out with my eyes or any sense the information that I really demand—and this although my eyes are keener than ever, my senses, as it seems to me, freed from certain bonds by which, I remember, they used to be both bounded and distorted.

The same strangeness is spread like a stain over my memory. Not that I have the slightest difficulty in recalling every incident, and with the greatest detail, from the period of time during which I was alive. But in spite of this clarity with which I present the actions of the past to the mind's eye, there is invariably something lacking in each picture that I see, some gap or intermission, not in the vision, but in my appreciation of it, as though in each sharply defined scene the figure that wears my own face is actually a stranger, and the people with whom I observe myself interchanging words, thoughts or caresses are ghosts or the figments of a dream. Yet it would appear that both dreams and ghosts can own a vitality far stronger than one suspected, for I am continually questioning these living things, uneasy with myself until I find an answer to what most perplexes me. What was the meaning or purpose of the voices and the show, I ask? and over and over again I demand, myself perhaps a mere symbol, 'Why was it that I was killed?'

There is one exception which I must make to what I have said already about the vividness of the impressions which I retain from the past. The very last scene of all, though clear enough in its main outline, is vague in certain respects. The exact locality of the battle in which I lost my life still, for some reason, evades me, although, strangely enough, there have been many occasions on which I have been listening to old soldiers and comrades in arms when I have been momentarily convinced that I had identified the place and the campaign. To one of them I may say 'I passed you on the way to the front line. You were engaged in some repair work on your lorry and raised your head and grinned as we went past.' To another I recall with perfect confidence the time when he was sitting with a group of friends beneath an enormous tree with scarlet flowers at a curious café in some foreign town. Yet later on I begin to doubt the precise accuracy of these recollections. Was it really these faces that I noticed on the way to the final clash, or others like them? Most confusing also is the fact that when I hear these men speak of their campaigns they are all familiar to me, so that it seems that I must have done impossible things such as fighting at the same time in two widely separated localities.

It is easy to imagine that my uncertainty on these important details adds greatly to my main perplexity; for, obviously, if I am to answer accurately the question that most troubles me—'Why was I killed?'—it is desirable to have the most precise information about the events which led up immediately to the last act.

One thing I can remember perfectly, and that is that just before going into action I had received a letter from my wife. She was, when she wrote, expecting a baby in about a month's time, and I wondered whether by the time the letter reached me the child might not actually be born. It was a prospect that made me glad, for up to then we had had no children.

The letter made me feel homesick for a time. I resented being away from my family in this distant place, and began to wish either that the war had never started, or that we had won it already. In a way I was glad to be going into action now, for we were all keyed up for the attack and it seemed that a success might have some finality about it. We wanted to get the thing over. It did not occur to me then that I should be killed.

And now again I curse the queer tricks which my memory plays upon me. I remember the roar of gunfire and the exact location of each battery. I remember the sweep past of the big new tanks that went into action in front of us, the roar of engines in the sky, and the dull or eager faces of the men on each side of me as we lay waiting for the word in shallow trenches below the escarpment. Yet, for some reason, the details of the landscape, though I see them vividly enough, are disconnected and inconsistent. Sometimes I see dunes of sand and the fighters above them in a clear sky; sometimes the ground appears covered in snow; sometimes we wade through mud that clings to our ankles. I remember long stretches of empty ground, and also trees torn by blast and the walls of houses crumbling under gunfire. I was in one of these scenes, or in all of them, and this is all of which I am certain.

My memory of the moment of attack is sharp enough: how we scrambled to our feet and went forward at a run through the shell-bursts. I was half-conscious of the dull vibration of the ground which seemed a kind of dismal accompaniment to the sudden roar of bomb-bursts, and the scream of shells. To left and right of me I observed men stumble, fling out their arms and fall. Then in a moment, without any special noise or excitement, what I had often thought about but never clearly imagined took place. It seemed, I think, that the ground quivered and I was conscious of the very slightest pang of nausea. Then it was all over, in a simple way, almost as though someone had pulled over me a black cloth. Indeed there was something uncannily beautiful about the speed, precision and finality of it. Immediately I knew that I had been killed, for I could see my own body, with the trouser legs torn and the knot in the bootlace that I had broken that morning. It was lying away from me so that I looked down the chest towards the feet and upturned boots. I could not see my face.

And my first feeling at that moment was so overpowering that it has remained fixed in me, nor do I see yet how I shall be rid of it. For just at the crux of time which marked my death I saw momentarily with two visions. I saw my body extending a little way over the shattered ground, and the boots with the broken bootlace, but I seemed to see also with the eyes of the face that was invisible and which were upturned upon a quite different view. What they perceived was the rounded summit of a hill as it might be seen across a valley by one lying on his back on the turf and thyme. Over and around the grassy slopes was a sky of the purest blue and at a great height some small clouds gently driven by a summer breeze. They and one bird that slowly on heavy wings was crossing the profound expanse seemed to add both height and depth to the scene so that the heaven was made more boundless than I had ever envisaged it, although the hill with its grassy slopes and sheep straying upon them was near, familiar and inviting, seen with such clarity and distinction that there was associated with the sight all the sounds of water breaking in the valley stream, animals bleating on the upper pastures, the very touch and texture of the grass and small flowers among the grass, the smell of earth and blossom, stone, water, the whole of summer brought over miles and miles of country by the straying intermittent breeze.

All this, in the least moment of time, was seen by the dead face which I could not see, and, impossible as the thing may seem, at this very same moment I saw the churned-up battlefield, the stained uniform which I wore, the lifeless and foolish legs. These two simultaneous visions soon melted away from me, and became an experience in the memory, but the strangeness, almost the impossibility, of the experience was such that I was profoundly affected by it, and filled immediately with the severest feelings of despondency and foreboding.

I saw in a moment how unutterably splendid was the whole depth and array of life, how limitless were its horizons, how sweetly thrilling were its humblest aspects. Yet all this I had looked upon as though through the frosted panes of glass in a small room, barely venturing from time to time on an attempt to extend my vision until now the glass was shattered and, too late, I could see it all. Now my body was lying on the disrupted ground, and to its left and right, behind and before, in all quarters of the globe, beneath the sea and under masses of masonry were others in a like case, who had not reached this condition of inertia of their own accord nor wholly by accident. 'Why was I killed?' I asked myself, and the question fell with such weight and precision upon my mind that its stamp has been indelible. I knew that I could not rest until I had done my utmost to provide an answer.

To some, no doubt, this question of mine may appear unnecessary, already answered, or merely selfish. 'It is over now,' they will say, 'why bother about the past? The milk is spilt.' Or they will tell me that I was killed in order to resist aggression or to promote freedom. 'Who am I?' it may well be asked. 'Who am I to make a fuss, an anonymous drop in the ocean of so much destruction?'

Certainly the questions are justified, the statement is accurate. It was, no doubt, the strangeness of my

experience at the moment of death which has led me
to approach the whole question in a way that differs
somewhat from the normal. What most disturbs my
mind is the past that I did not know and which has
not departed. I am inclined to doubt whether the origin
of so great a slaughter, both of friend and foe, can be
discovered only in diplomatic documents or by the
consideration of various schools of thought; and I can
assure my questioners that I am perfectly aware of my
own insignificance in history. It is when I think of
my own case as multiplied by a million and by ten
million that it begins to appear a matter of some
importance. Years ago it was some such a one as I who
was buried in half the capitals of the world, unknown
soldiers whose burial places were held in peculiar
veneration.

CHAPTER I

The Sightseers

In one of these places I now stand on the cold stone. It is the aisle of some great abbey or cathedral. In the dim light of early afternoon the array of tattered colours, once prized by distinguished regiments of the dead, hang limp and scarcely substantial, like rows of cobwebs from the high vault, and lead the eye to an enormous cross of gold that stands above a neat and whitely furnished altar above which a red lamp is glowing. In front of this altar I observe the figure of a man dressed in clerical robes. He is on his knees in an attitude of prayer, and soon I begin to hear mumbled words, though for some time I cannot accustom my ear sufficiently well to his accents to be able to determine their sense. My impulse is to approach more closely to him and, as I take a step forward, I uncover a portion of the stone on which I have been standing. The inscription reads: 'TO THE UNKNOWN SOLDIER,' and I can see also a fragment of the date which was carved on the stone at the time when it was first set in place. I can see, that is, the figures 'one' and 'nine,' but now my whole

18

attention is distracted so that I cannot say whether the tomb on which I stand commemorates the last great war or the one in which I myself lost my life, or even some other conflict which may have broken out subsequently. Nor is this a problem which much concerns me at the moment, for now I can hear distinctly the words which the priest is speaking. 'Give eternal peace,' he says, 'to all those, of whatever nation, of whatever creed, of whatever colour, of whatever education, occupation and financial status, who have lost their lives in the land, on the sea or in the air.'

As he speaks a thin shaft of sunlight pierces past me through a high window, lights up the tattered banners and sinks into a patch of brilliant white on the surplice that covers the shoulders of the kneeling man. I bow my head in respect for the dignity of the words and the occasion, and I see the large shadow of my head on the cold stone before me. Yet although for the moment I am impressed by the clergyman's invocation of eternal peace, I am still conscious of my perplexity and even, unwarrantable as this may be, of a certain indignation; for I am perfectly aware that I am not at peace. One question is still uppermost in my mind and, as I feel again its impress, I step forward and approach the priest.

He must have heard my footsteps, for, as I move towards him, he rises from his knees and turns to face me. I notice at once that I was deceived in my first judgment of him. From the back he had seemed to have a slender and youthful figure, but his face is the face of an old man, a kind face, I consider, with much resolution about the mouth, although the deep lines on his forehead and along his cheeks denote mental suffering of great intensity, and the deepset eyes, though sympathetic, are piercing.

Evidently he is surprised to see me, and I myself feel some embarrassment at my rudeness in so interrupting his devotions. Yet I speak first and say: 'Why was it that all those men of whom you were speaking lost their lives?'

He looks straight in my eyes for a moment, almost seeming as if he is surprised that such a question should be asked at all. 'Was it the will of God?' I ask again, and I see him turn his head quickly to the large golden cross that is spread high over the altar at which he has been praying. He looks down again to the ground and tomb where I am standing. 'No,' he says, 'it was the will of man,' and I believe that he is going to continue speaking; but now we are interrupted by the noise of the closing of a heavy door in some other part of the building and by the sound of footsteps approaching us over the stones. Voices too are audible and in particular one voice that is raised as though in exhortation.

Both the priest and I move to one of the arches at the side of the chapel in which we stand. Through this arch we can observe a party of sightseers who are being conducted by a guide to the historic monuments of the place. This guide is a small and old man, somewhat crooked in the back. He is wearing a black robe or cassock of some sort so that he appears to hold some higher rank than that to which actually he belongs. His is the voice, surprisingly strong and resonant for so small a body, which I noticed before was upraised above the rest.

The party seem to be gathered about some object against the wall farthest from which I stand. Now I can hear distinctly the words spoken by the guide. 'Here lies,' he is saying, 'one of the most distinguished of those who took part in the second crusade. You can tell from the position of the legs of the effigy that it was the second rather than the first or third.' I can hear the little man's stick tap twice or thrice upon the sculptured legs. 'If,' he continues, 'the man himself was as large physically as is the effigy, he must have been a fighting man of no mean prowess.'

A murmur of approval greets this declaration, and the group of visitors with their guide begins to move towards the chapel where the priest and I are standing. I can hear the voice of a young man speaking to a girl who clings close to his arm as though the size and solemnity of the building have inspired in her a sort of dismay so that she needs support and reassurance. 'Of course,' the young man is saying, 'those crusades were all very well, but they didn't come to much. Actually I believe that they caused a great deal of disease.'

And now I can see the whole group of people who are drifting and shuffling, rather as corks or sticks upon a slow current than as if with deliberate intent, into the small chapel below the thin and motionless flags. Their guide bustles behind them, pointing them to the place where he would have them be. His black dress and the long stick with which he taps the stones seem to invest him with a kind of authority over his charges who turn their heads inquisitively and purposelessly to all quarters of the enormous building. He seems like some shabby Mercury escorting the perplexed parties of the dead to their final resting place, while they stare about them at the unusual scenery, having heard mentioned previously the sights which they see, but never having come before on this road.

I see that there are six persons with this guide. There are the young man and girl whom I have mentioned already; there is an elderly bearded man of scholarly appearance; also a man of middle age, whose stubborn indignant face interests me strangely, since it occurs to me at once that I have seen it before. There is a woman who must be about the age of my own mother: her close-fitting black dress appears somehow to constrain and isolate her, so that she seems remote from, though not indifferent to the others. I observe particularly the whiteness of her hands and the fact that her face shows traces of recent tears. Then there is a man dressed wealthily, tall, somewhat stout, with a powerful and confident air. I should guess him to be, or to have been, a person of some influence in the world.

The voices of these people are hushed as they enter the chapel, which inspires them, it seems, with a peculiar reverence. I notice that the woman in black raises, for a moment, her handkerchief to her face, and that the prosperous-looking person stands for a brief instant at attention.

And now the guide begins to speak. 'This chapel,' he says, 'has been visited by many millions of persons. It is dear to us all, and not least dear to our friends from overseas. It commemorates the Unknown Soldier. Now the curious thing about this is that no one, not even the highest authorities, knows who he is.'

The young girl sighs and says 'How beautiful!' She

is somewhat shocked by the remark of the man on whose arm she leans. 'It wouldn't make a lot of difference to the poor chap anyway,' he says. 'I mean, if anyone knew anything about him. I mean obviously it wouldn't.'

The bearded man, whom I have imagined to be a scholar, speaks in a voice whose accents differ somewhat from the voices of the rest. 'Anonymity,' he says, 'it is an imposition,' and he looks startled as he observes that the others have failed to understand his sentence. 'I would say that it imposes itself,' he adds, and the young girl clutches him by the arm. 'You mean "imposing," ' she whispers. He bows and smiles. 'Imposing, I thank you heartily, imposing. It places, I would say, an emphasis.'

The man whom I have guessed to be prosperous now speaks in a rich and confident voice. 'You are right, sir,' he says. 'Anonymity is right. It is the common man everywhere who counts in the long run. They do their duty. It is a very good show, on the whole. Theirs, I mean to say, not to reason why.' Here he coughs and begins to look embarrassed.

The young man is laughing, and I observe that once more the woman in the black dress has raised her handkerchief to her eyes. I notice too that there is a particularly grim expression on the face of that middle-aged and obstinate-looking man whom I fancy that I have recognized. 'When we were in Spain . . .' he begins, but he has not time to finish his sentence, for now the priest steps forward from my side and the sound of his shoes upon the hard stone attracts for the first time the attention of the group to him and me.

He speaks in a way that, although surprising, is extremely gratifying to me.

'Supposing,' he says, 'my friends—and the idea is of course preposterous, quite absurd—but supposing just for the sake of argument that we, you and I, were to meet this unknown soldier, and supposing that he, being, let us assume, an inquisitive and imaginative man, were to ask us straight out "Why was I killed?" —what sort of answer do you think that we should give him?'

CHAPTER II

The Argument

I saw then that the group of men and women appeared to be both embarrassed and discouraged by the clergyman's question. Some raised their hands to their mouths and coughed; others turned their heads aside as though they had suddenly discovered elsewhere some object of absorbing interest. The priest spoke again.

'Of course,' he said, 'I am well aware that I am addressing you in a most unusual way. I will tell you why I do so. Just now, before you came in, there was a soldier here. He looked, I thought, an intelligent man, and he asked me this very question.'

Now I saw that the priest and the whole group of people were looking straight at me, but what was astonishing was that none of them, it seemed, could see me, although I myself could distinguish clearly the shadow of my head upon the stone and, if I had extended my hand ever so little, I should have touched the arm of the priest who stood beside me. But I could not just then dwell upon my surprise at finding myself invisible, nor attempt to explain the fact. My attention was drawn to the tall and wealthy man who, swaying slightly on his heels, pronounced these words in a firm voice.

'I should say, sir, quite definitely, that one would reply more or less as follows. One would say this to the fellow quite simply. "You were killed for your country. Your country was in peril. You and many others answered the call, and this time, as in the past, you put up a remarkably fine show. We are proud of you, sir." '

While he was speaking he looked directly into my eyes so that I saw most distinctly his fat, but powerful, face, and found it more than ever incomprehensible that he, apparently, was wholly unaware of my presence. At the conclusion of his speech, he lowered his eyes to the ground and began nervously to finger his tie. I received the impression that in spite of his apparent confidence, he was embarrassed by what he had said and somewhat fearful that his views would not receive the approval of the others. As for me, I could attach very little meaning to the words which he had pronounced. Not that they were untrue, but their truth seemed irrelevant when I set it beside the two scenes which I had observed at the moment of my death— that sunny hillside and the broken arms and legs. I was glad to hear the priest speak again.

'I see what you mean,' he said, 'but it is possible that this soldier of ours' (and here he looked directly at me) 'would not understand you perfectly. After all we do not know even whether he was in the fullest sense one of our own countrymen. He may have come from some distant quarter of the globe and never have seen our great cities or our monuments. We do not know whether or not he believed in the justice of our cause. We know nothing except that he was killed fighting.'

I looked round from face to face of the group of sightseers, wondering how they had been affected by the priest's words; and I was glad to see both interest and attention in their manner. It appeared that they had by now recovered from the shock of the strangeness and unconventionality of the question (though to me the question had seemed both natural and worth a considered reply) and now they were busy with their thoughts, critical, as I had been, of the words of the first speaker, who himself, I thought, was not wholly convinced that he had hit the nail upon the head. His feet were shuffling somewhat uneasily, though he had thrust his jaw forward, as if determined to defend his thesis.

Almost at once he was forced to do so. The young man, to whose arm the girl was still clinging, stepped a little way in front of the circle. I looked closely at the pair of them and considered that they were both younger than they had seemed at first sight. The man's face was intelligent, but rather too lean and sharply peaked. There was a fixed glimmer of what might have been defiance or resentment in his eyes, although he would smile often and no doubt would have the reputation of a wit among his friends. The girl was pale and pretty without being beautiful. It was evident that she was a person of no great independence, however affectionate might be her nature, and she clung to the young man's arm with a rapacious and uneasy devotion. He addressed himself abruptly to the last speaker.

'Look here, cock,' he said, 'I don't know what your name is, but . . .'

'Fothey, my dear sir,' replied the prosperous looking man immediately. 'F O T H E Y , Fothey.' He bowed slightly and, on straightening his back, began nervously to pat the top of his head with his left hand.

He bowed again when the girl, looking at him fiercely, said '*His* name's Mr. Clark, Bob Clark.' She turned her head and smiled proudly at her escort, who appeared somewhat taken aback by these introductions, and to have for the moment lost the thread of his discourse. After a short pause he began again. 'Well, Mr. Fothey,' he said, 'or Lord Fothey . . .'

'Sir Alfred Fothey, as a matter of fact,' replied the other. Again he showed his embarrassment by patting furiously the top of his head. He looked imploringly at the young man, who again was at a loss for words. After a pause he added sadly: 'Yes, Sir Alfred Fothey. You may have heard of my young cousin, perhaps. He was a cricketer.'

Bob Clark now spoke again. 'Well,' he said, 'Sir Alfred Fothey. Got it right this time.' He grinned at the girl. 'What I was going to say when I was interrupted . . .'

'I beg your pardon, I'm sure, my dear fellow,' interjected Sir Alfred.

'Don't mention it, cock. What I was going to say was that you really must come off it. All this patriotism stuff, I mean, and "do or die" and all the rest of it. It's all bunk. You're behind the times, old boy. That's about it.'

Sir Alfred appeared more embarrassed than ever, although it was clear that many of the group of people sympathized with him and approved of what he had said. He looked at the priest as though for reassurance, but the priest was staring at the ground, indeed at my feet, though it seemed that he could not see them.

After coughing and looking once round the group of sightseers, Sir Alfred replied hesitantly, but in a manner that showed that he was convinced of the truth of what he said. 'Come, come, my dear sir,' he said. 'I may be old-fashioned, but you cannot make me believe that patriotism is dead. We have signal examples of it every day. We cannot but be proud of our heritage.'

Here the young man nudged the girl in the side with his elbow and winked. I could not but feel sorry for Sir Alfred who was stumbling over his words. I could see what was in his mind's eye—views of rolling country, lakes and rivers, libraries of books, old buildings, marching feet, recollections of history, dignity and leisure— yet he was incapable of putting into words the strong feelings of pride, reverence and delight with which these scenes were associated in his mind. He concluded rather lamely.

'No doubt, Mr. Clark, I expressed myself badly. The idea is more or less what somebody put into poetry. I mean "The game is more than the player of the game and the ship is more than the crew!" ' He coughed nervously before his face took on again its habitual expression of resolution; but I had seen enough of him to know that behind the dignified façade was much sensitivity, a rather pathetic desire to please, a bewilderment which I had not previously imagined as characteristic of the class of men to which Sir Alfred belonged.

'Now see here, Sir Alfred Fothey,' said the young man. 'Listen to me, because I *know*. I've had plenty of pals who went out there.' And he waved his hand vaguely in my direction. 'Plenty of them; and I can tell you that if you started talking to them about ships and crews and players and the rest, then you'd be lucky if they only laughed. When I think of this unknown soldier we're supposed to be talking about, I think of my pals and of myself, since I'd have had to go too if I hadn't been in munitions. And all this stuff of yours makes me sick. Justice-of-our-cause my aunt Fanny! Our glorious heritage! So what? Where is it? Someone will always have to work, I suppose. To the chaps on top, of course, it makes a difference whether *they're* on top or someone else. But to the chaps underneath it isn't all that important. Hardly worth getting killed for. Of course when the enemy start dropping bombs on us, and a lot of people get bombed-out, and when we read in the papers that some of our fellows who are prisoners are getting badly treated, then that makes a number of chaps wild and they want to go and do something about it. And the fellows on the other side are probably feeling the same. It's all done by propaganda, really, and nobody knows what the whole thing's about. All we know is that there's more work and better money for those who are lucky. Don't get the idea that I'm a pacifist or anything like that. If they send for you you've got to go. You can't get away from that. But the ordinary man would much rather stay at home, and everyone knows it, however much you may talk about "answering the call," etc., etc. The call comes through the post and nobody's particularly pleased when he gets it. But you can't pick and choose. It would be a funny sort of world if you could. You've just got to go where you're sent. So if this soldier asked me why he was killed, I'd think he was a bit soft. He got killed because he got hit with something. That's all there is about it. He was one of the unlucky ones. It was tough on him, but he couldn't help that. But I wouldn't make him mad by talking about his glorious heritage or pretending that he was a sort of hero or anything.'

Bob Clark paused and licked his lips. Sir Alfred was in a state of considerable agitation and was beating the top of his head with his hand extended like a rapidly moving flipper. 'My dear sir,' he said, 'my dear sir, I hardly think you can be aware where these ideas will lead you.'

The young man grinned. 'That's all right, cock,' he replied. 'I don't expect they'll lead anywhere. And besides they're not ideas. They're facts.' He looked down to the girl at his side, who nodded her head emphatically. She spoke nervously and seriously as though she were repeating a lesson learnt by heart.

'What people want really,' she said, 'is really a nice little home.'

I looked from one to the other of them, and knew that much of what had been said was true. Yet what truth there had been in the words spoken did nothing to decrease my perplexity and discouragement. There was more, I knew, in life than would be contained in the type of home which the girl envisaged. There was more too than mechanical compulsion behind the actions of those whom I had known at the battle front. Not many of them had enjoyed fighting or even volunteered for this activity; not many had had any great faith in or affection for the authorities who had set them tasks in which their lives were lost; yet most had been willing to perform these tasks; most had been convinced, at one time or another, that their action and their sacrifice were in some way valuable, that, as a result of the carnage, some better state of affairs would, somehow or other, emerge. It was true that we had no wish to regard ourselves as heroes, but neither for long could we bear the thought that we might be mere automata, dragooned by some incomprehensible force into performing dangerous actions whose results were meaningless.

I saw that Sir Alfred was on the point of speaking again and that several others were about to expostulate or agree with Bob Clark's answer to my question; but before any of them had a chance to speak the priest once more intervened. He was looking directly at me in such a way that I found it hard to believe that he was unaware of my presence, and when he spoke he seemed to be addressing his words as much to me as to the others. He spoke slowly.

'It may well be that this soldier of whom we are speaking had little or no choice in adopting the course which led to his being killed. But just this fact alone would not satisfy him. Nor is it in itself by any means a criticism of the value of what he may have achieved or wished to achieve. I think he would like to be sure that, however it was that he met his end, there was some worthy purpose in it all, that he had helped to achieve something really notable, that there was a deeper necessity than any which you have yet mentioned.

Remember that we have to imagine this soldier as dead, and, however, frequently we may read or hear of death, it is an experience which none of us can precisely envisage. Its uniqueness, its finality, its importance are things which we know, but cannot estimate. This is true of all death and perhaps particularly true of the deaths of those who, like this soldier, have in all probability died young, before their time. Moreover he did not die in any way which can be properly called either natural or accidental. He was placed deliberately in a position where death was much more than ordinarily frequent, and he inflicted on others what in the end he met himself. Whether he was conscious of it or not at the time, the sacrifice which he made was real and final; for he gave up not only his past but his future, great possibilities which he may not yet have been able to imagine. He would be most inhuman who would not demand that this sacrifice should be worth the making.'

The priest's words had been uttered slowly and tentatively, almost as if he had been speaking in his sleep. He had kept his eyes fixed on me and I was surprised at the accuracy of his analysis of my present state of mind. Not that it was wholly accurate, for the word 'sacrifice' conveyed little meaning to me, nor had I, as he seemed to imagine I should have, any feelings of guilt for the fact that I had been instrumental in procuring for others the same fate which I had myself suffered. Feelings such as these I had had in the past, but they were now stamped from my mind by the vigour of the impression of the moment of death. That sunny valley and beautiful vision: what I had not known was what most affected my mind, and I knew that no easy answer would satisfy my perplexity; yet among the answers which I sought was certainly the assurance that my death had not, in the long run, been as meaningless as had been, I now perceived, too much of my life.

I saw step forward from the group of people the scholarly man with the imperfect knowledge of our language. I had guessed him to be a refugee, political or racial, from some other country. His eyes flashed as he spoke, stumbling often over his words, and, as he fingered his beard with one hand, he would glance quickly from side to side, nervously, as if, in spite of the confidence of his speech, he was fearful of opposition and anxious to find himself voicing the opinion of the majority.

'Forgive me, gentlemen,' he said, 'and ladies, but it is too obvious; at least so I think. Surely I believe. What he knows, what he does not know, how does it matter? We do not know too much. No one. But what he does, there it is. He defends us all. He saves many from terrible things, from the barbarities, from the prison. He defends culture, civilization, the progress. This is not a real thing? No? It is very real. I could tell you, I am sorry, how real it is. He is dead to resist the evil idea. He did not aggress, but he defended. It was very good.'

I saw that several of the others nodded their heads in agreement with what the old scholar had said, and that he himself was pleased with the recognition which he had secured. Yet the next one of the party to speak was in evident disagreement.

'Defend, defend, defend,' came the voice. 'We have heard too much of it. What have we defended? What have we that is worth defending? No, old friend. I fancy that you are barking up the wrong tree.'

The speaker was that middle-aged man with the firm and stubborn face whom previously I had noticed in particular. Something about his bearing, the uprightness of it, or perhaps merely the old mackintosh buttoned up to his chin gave him a soldierly appearance, and I had felt, as soon as I had seen him, that in all probability he would have a fuller understanding, not perhaps of my predicament but certainly of the events which had led up to it, than would most of the others of the party. I saw now that he was smiling on the old refugee who had been put greatly out of countenance by the sudden outburst of dissent.

'Forgive me, sir,' he said, 'if I spoke too abruptly.'

'For nothing,' replied the scholar. 'I would wish to reflect upon your views.'

The soldier, for so I took him to be, set his feet apart, undid the top button of his mackintosh, and folded his hands behind his back. He looked sharply round the circle of sightseers, and began to speak quickly and precisely. I saw that he was perhaps unique among these people in having already arranged his ideas on this subject and in not having to speak, as had most of the others, entirely on the spur of the moment.

'What I have to contribute to this discussion,' he said, 'is perhaps rather more definite than what has been said hitherto. Imagine that this man' (here he glanced quickly at me, but without appearing to see me) 'imagine that this man asks us: "Why was I killed?" Leaving aside all sentiment, I think we could give him a straight answer to a straight question. Personally I should say to him, "You were killed because of the folly and incapacity of your own government," and if he wanted further detail, I should give him dates, places, speeches and personalities. In particular I should refer him to the meetings of the so-called Non-Intervention Committee which I regard as having aided and abetted the slaughter of many of my own friends and having paved the way for a much greater slaughter. I know that it is fashionable now to say "recriminations about the past are useless," but this is not an argument which I have yet heard put forward by a murderer in his defence in a court of law. In the commission of any crime there may be extenuating circumstances; but the crime is none the less committed.

'This, then, would be my first and most direct answer to our unknown soldier. There have been many wars which no skill or foresight could have avoided. This was not one of those. The best we can say is that we lacked the skill and foresight.

'But I am aware that this answer would not satisfy him. It might well be that he himself had approved all the actions of his own government which led directly to his own death. He would still, as you have said, wish to be reassured that his death was not entirely meaningless. And this reassurance, I am afraid, can only be given him by the future and by the living. If we attempt to satisfy him by informing him that he died for freedom, for culture, for civilization, for what Sir Alfred has described as "our glorious heritage," it is quite possible that he might reply, as Mr. Clark would perhaps reply, "What freedom? What culture? What glorious heritage?" If we appeal to his humanitarianism and try to persuade him that he died in order to save others from the horrors of a concentration camp, it is possible that he might be one who, like myself, is aware that concentration camps are not the monopoly of any particular race or creed, that, moreover, many of the first and bravest of his own allies have perished miserably in the prisons of those who all the time were vociferating that they shared their ideals. If we appeal to his love for culture, it may be that he is one who never had the time or opportunity to equip himself for such pleasures.

'No, no, my friends! Are we ourselves certain that to defend the state of affairs that existed before the war was worth all that blood? Of course we are not; and it was with this in mind that I objected to our friend's use of the word "defence," and that I suggest that we ourselves from a consideration of the past are totally unable to give this soldier a satisfactory answer. If he ever receives such an answer it will come, I say, not from *us*, but from the future.

'So far as our own knowledge goes, all we can say to him is that he was fortunate or unfortunate enough to be born at a period when the slow forces of necessity were in the act of producing a new form of society and a new type of man. It was a kind of production of which his rulers knew little or nothing. He could not have been blinder than they were to the realities of the situation. Yet the realities were there. There were ideals, there were possibilities which deserved not only defence but active fighting for their furtherance.

'So far as his death contributed to those possibilities

he may regard it as immensely valuable. Certainly he fought oppression; but, with oppression so ubiquitous, it is not difficult to do that. We may fairly imagine, too, that he shared in the comradeship of battle, that he felt bound to his fellows by the strong tie of mutual danger and endeavour—a feeling which is like, but not precisely the same as that which Sir Alfred mentioned. Yet his opponents also had these feelings and knew this comradeship. It is not worth the expense of blood merely to promote by war a fine emotion that is too rare in times of peace. Nor even would his death be worth while if it merely helped to restore to bombed and invaded districts the uneasy tranquillity which they enjoyed before the first shot was fired.

'It is something more positive than defence or restoration which he would wish to have served. "A new world," "a world fit for heroes"—these are phrases which have unfortunate associations, yet they express practical necessities. It is in the fight for such a world rather than in any form of defence that killing may be justified, and it is we alone who can perform the justification. We have imagined this dead man as anxious to discover some value in his death; but by himself he can never discover it; it is we who must give it to him.'

He stopped speaking, shut his jaws tightly, like a trap, and looked round from one to the others of his hearers. He had spoken with vehemence and assurance, and the very force of his conviction seemed for the moment to have subdued the rest. I saw that Bob Clark again winked and smiled at the girl, though whether the gesture was in approbation of a vigorous speech or in corroboration of its sentiments I could not determine. Sir

Alfred Fothey was slowly rubbing the back of his head, which he nodded up and down.

I noticed that the priest kept his eyes fixed upon the elderly woman in black, whose white face and slender hands I had particularly noticed. I imagined her to be a widow, or one who had lost a son or a brother in the war; for she had seemed more affected than the others by the place in which she stood, and from time to time she would raise her handkerchief to her face. She had been listening intently to the argument, but it had not been the argument itself so much as events of which it had reminded her that had moved her feelings. She now began to speak, keeping her eyes upon the priest, from whom, it seemed, she imagined that she could expect more understanding than from the others.

'It's wrong,' she said, 'and especially in this place to talk politics. It wasn't really this or that government's fault that he was killed; it was all *our* fault. And your fine ideas may sound good, but they can't alter nature. There are fine things in nature too, but they don't come out finely in the end. We trust in God; we do our duty; we love our husbands and our sons; but still we can't keep them, and often the best things in them are the things which take them away from us. I am afraid I cannot speak well and clearly like you do: but when I think of how a mother loves her baby, and holds it close to her, and how, later on, she is sometimes proud to see the same baby grown up, wearing a uniform, ready to kill and be killed; when I think of how our men, however they may love us, are ready to leave us and die for some kind of an idea which they themselves do not understand, and how we admire them for this, and would not have them different; when I think of these simple things, and then hear you speak of oppression and oppressors, I say to myself, "we are the oppressors; our best and dearest feelings lead us to our deaths." All we want is love, a home, children, security. Suppose we have all these. Fear of loss will poison each of them, and we know that what are considered most sacred feelings of duty and loyalty will help to do away with them. I think sometimes that we do not want to live, and that it will take more than politics to cure this.'

Here she turned away from the priest and looked straight at me.

'This soldier,' she said. 'I would tell him that he died for the sins of the whole world. He meant no harm. Nor did we. But we all killed him, and he killed himself.'

She spread out her hands in an appealing gesture. 'I cannot make myself plain,' she added, 'but it is something in nature.'

The man in the mackintosh threw out his hand impatiently, but before he could speak the priest intervened.

'I think I understand you,' he said, 'and I think that this soldier of ours would understand you if he could see you as I do.' Here he paused and looked fixedly at me. He began to speak again, slowly and almost as though he were measuring the effect of his words upon me. 'But our words by themselves,' he was saying, 'might well be most misleading. What trivial things they are when taken from the whole context of our lives together! For our arguments on this subject are nothing like mathematics and cannot tend to any proof or to much certainty. They are parts of ourselves, nothing abstract, facets of our own experience and of the experience of others. And we ourselves, all our experiences, are connected each to each. This soldier's life and death are parts of us, as we are parts of him. How much better it would be if, instead of listening to our conversation, he could see our past, our present, even our future—the stuff of which our arguments are made. If he could do so, I wonder whether he would see a greater unanimity and more comfort than there has been in our words.'

He paused and looked upwards at the grey and draggling flags. The sun now shone strongly and pierced their tissues so as to make them appear insubstantial webs in air. I saw that Sir Alfred Fothey had begun to speak.

'It's true,' he was saying, 'that this is a difficult subject.' But I did not immediately hear the words that were to follow. Though his face was still in front of me, I was myself in a quite different scene, and my eyes were focussed on nothing that was in the abbey, but upon the long and dripping boughs of evergreen trees which fringed a winding drive of gravel up which I was walking towards a large and brightly lighted house.

CHAPTER III

So Were They All

1

THE windows, both on the ground, the first and the second floor were indeed blazing with light. My feet crunched on the gravel as I walked between the wet trees to the front door of the house. I was walking rapidly, as if with a set purpose, although in point of fact I had no notion whatever as to why I was making this visit. More strange still, perhaps, I was conscious of no surprise at finding myself suddenly in quite different surroundings, and this although I remembered clearly the faces and the words of the sightseers whom I had just left. Indeed, impossible as it may seem, I could still see them, or at least was fully conscious of their presence, so that I was now, it appeared, in two places and perhaps in two times at once. Nor did I find anything unnatural or impossible in this.

I came to the front door and entered, passing into a large hall, the walls of which were adorned with various trophies, assegais and cutlasses, the heads of buffaloes, bisons and antelopes. A tiger-skin extended over

the floor in front of a brisk fire of logs, and from a
room opening out of a hall to my left I could hear the
hum of voices, laughter and the twanging of a guitar.
Something in the atmosphere of the place—whether it
was the warmth and brightness of the fire, the cleanli-
ness and order of the ornaments on the mantel-shelf, or
the confident merriness of the voices—impressed me with
a feeling of geniality, security, and repose such as I had
never known.

I looked up and saw descending the wide staircase in
front of me a tall and beautiful woman, whose appearance at once surprised me, for her clothes were like none
which I had ever seen, but reminded me of the pictures
in old books which I used to read in my childhood—
pictures of the men and women who lived sixty or
seventy years ago.

The lady reached the bottom of the stairs and, as she
walked slowly towards me, I took a step forward to meet
her, being uncertain as to how I should explain my
appearance here, and yet strangely unembarrassed by
the evident necessity for doing so. She looked directly
into my eyes, smiling very sweetly, but without showing
the least awareness of my presence, so that I realized
once more that I was invisible to her, and I stepped
aside to let her pass towards the door on my left.

The door was opened before she reached it, and there
came out into the hall a young man wearing a military
uniform of antique type. His whiskers and moustache
too were such as I had never seen except in pictures.
His handsome face was smiling as he advanced towards
the lady and took her hands in his; but as he passed
me I noticed that the shadow of my head fell full across

his face, and he turned quickly, as though momentarily startled, in my direction. I saw that now there were tears in the lady's eyes.

'Jack,' she said. 'They tell me you got a special message. When are you going?'

He had looked away from me now, and was smiling. 'To-night, mother,' he said, and then, noticing her distress, he put one arm about her waist, and kissed her on the forehead. 'You mustn't mind,' he said. 'Soon I'll be sending you rugs and carpets and shawls and all the things they have out there. And, who knows, I may be made a general even younger than father was.'

He laughed and she, seeing him do so, forced a smile. They went past me towards the room on the left, and I followed them to the open doorway where we stood unobserved for the moment by those within.

It was a large room and most opulently furnished. Men were standing in groups or leaning over the backs of chairs and sofas where ladies were sitting with small cups of coffee in their hands. I noticed in particular an old man with grizzled hair, who was sitting on the arm of a large arm-chair by the fireplace. He was hale and vigorous, and, from the ease of his position and from the deference with which he seemed to be regarded by the rest, I took him to be the master of the house. He it was who had been strumming on the guitar, but now he had put the instrument down across his knees, and close to it, gently fingering one of the strings, stood a little boy of five or six years old, dressed again most oddly to my notions, whose face immediately interested me, since it reminded me of something which I had already seen.

The old man's face was grave. He was replying, it seemed, to a question which had been addressed to him by one of the guests. 'Yes, Harry,' he was saying, 'there's no doubt of it. Things are grave.' He shrugged his shoulders, while with one tough brown hand he smoothed the ends of his white moustache. 'Well,' he continued, 'what of it? Those fellows wanted war. Let them have it. That's what I say. It will be a lesson to them.'

One of the younger ladies who was sitting at some distance from the old man at the other side of the room began to speak in a thin and plaintive voice. 'But, Sir William,' she said, 'will there not be a terrible loss of life?'

Sir William looked sharply at her. 'Yes, my dear,' he replied. 'Yes, certainly. What of it? Our fellows aren't afraid to die. They're the right stuff.'

He turned his eyes suddenly to the doorway where I was standing with the lady whom I supposed to be his wife, and with their son. His face brightened as he saw the young man. He did not see me standing at his side.

'Hallo, Jack,' he said, 'I was just telling them that you young fellows are the right stuff. That's true of the Hussars, anyway, I know.'

The young man laughed. 'I hope so, sir,' he said, and as he moved forward, he attracted to himself the attention of all who were in the room.

There is, I know, something both exhilarating and disturbing in the presence at an ordinary gathering of one who is just about to go to the front, and I noticed now that, as the young man stepped forward towards his father's chair, the eyes of the others were fixed on him in a kind of uneasy admiration. The bearing of the young man himself, however gay and confident, was still tense. He walked up to the little boy at the old man's side, and gently rested his hand on his yellow hair. The little boy looked up at him and smiled. At the same time Sir William gripped him by the arm. 'Well, Alfred,' he said, 'are you proud of your big brother?'

Alfred slowly nodded his head. He turned to the old man and asked, 'Will he kill all the other soldiers?'

At this there was general laughter. Sir William slapped his knee and cried out, 'Hundreds of them, my dear fellow, hundreds and hundreds. They're regular devils, these Hussars. Used to be in my day, anyway. Cut and thrust. Cut and thrust. There's no doing anything with them, is there, my boy?'

The young man laughed again, while the little boy continued to gaze at him with awed and perplexed eyes. From my side the lady, his mother, stepped forward into the room.

'It's long past his bed time,' she said. 'Nanny is waiting for him.'

The boy turned appealing eyes towards his father, and the old man patted him reassuringly on the shoulder. 'Oh come!' he said. 'He must have a little extra leave. It's not every day that he can see his brother off to the wars. And I promised him a song, the little devil.'

'Yes, sir,' said the young man. 'Do sing him one; and then I'm afraid I shall have to say good-bye.'

At this, something of a hush fell upon the company. Sir William's face took on an air of gravity. 'Come, come,' he said, 'there's plenty of time.'

The young man shook his head. 'I've only just received the message,' he replied. 'I must be in the village in a quarter of an hour.'

Sir William nodded gravely and the young man smiled. 'So let's just hear one song,' he continued. 'It will be a good thing to remember you by.'

There was a murmur of approval from the guests. I noticed that the lady, who stood with her head turned slightly towards me, had raised, while still smiling, a hand to the corner of her eye. Sir William sighed, and with a quick gesture raised the guitar upon his knees and began to strum.

The little boy watched him with large and fascinated eyes, as his fingers moved over the strings, until finally, after clearing his throat once or twice, he began to sing a humorous song about a new shoe which pinched the foot of its wearer. Soon he began to warm to his subject. He winked, grimaced, and between the verses made facetious gestures appropriate to the sense of what he had sung, and I, as I looked round upon the faces of the contented smiling guests, on the wide-eyed delight of the little boy, on his brother's indulgent smile, and on the old man's spirited buffoonery, was impressed not only by the warmth and assurance of the scene, but also by a feeling of indescribable sadness, since I was so placed that I could see both the confident geniality of this gathering and also the instability of the bases upon which it rested. So I listened to the words of the song:

> *Tight shoe, don't bother me!*
> *Tight shoe, don't bother me!*
> *You squeal, you squeal, you squeal,*

Like a pig without a tail.
You squeal, you squeal, you squeal
Like an antediluvian whale.

and I smiled with the others, though with less confidence, as, when the song was over, the young man went round the room to shake hands with the guests and bid farewell to them. In front of me he stopped still for a moment and then went out into the hall with his arm round his mother's waist and his young brother clinging to his other hand. Sir William followed and I went out with them.

The young man received a sabre and military cloak from a butler who, having wished him well, retired. Sir William took his son's hand in a firm grip.

'Good-bye, my boy,' he said. 'God bless you. I've always been proud of you. Always. I know you'll do your duty.' His face stiffened into an expression of extreme severity, and then for a moment he turned his eyes away.

'I'll try to, sir,' said the young man. His jaw too was stiff and his whole body tensely held. He let go of his father's hand, embraced his mother, and lifted up the little boy to the level of his eyes. 'I'll see what I can bring you back, Alfred,' he said laughing, and the little boy, looking gravely at him, enquired 'How long?'

'Quite soon,' said his brother, and, smiling once more at his parents, he opened the door and went into the darkness outside.

Sir William put his arm round his wife's shoulders, and she rested her head against his sleeve. He remained staring fixedly at the door, which his son was closing from the outside. His face was drawn and pale, and, as the door shut, he turned quickly away, as though to avoid a sound that seemed final and irrevocable.

But I, as the door closed, saw beyond it, though not what I might have expected, the dark trees and the gravel drive. Instead I saw a sky of brilliant and dazzling blue, and below the sky a ridge of sand with sparse and desiccated bushes growing along its summit. Down from the ridge, in the middle distance, I could see a party of horsemen, trotting over a level expanse of hard and burning ground. From time to time one or other of them would look back towards the ridge where a riderless horse was standing, and at the horse's feet I saw, tumbled together and somehow abject in this immense wilderness, the body of a man. His right arm, grasping a sabre, was thrown out in front of him, and on the black hairs of his wrist I noticed a column of ants moving. They were climbing the sleeve and progressing to a point on his tunic which was soaked with blood. They and the distant group of horsemen were all that moved beneath the flashing sun. There was a stain of blood at the corner of the man's mouth, but I recognized him easily as the same whom I had just seen leaving the comfortable house. Was it his first charge, I wondered, in which he had fallen? Was it a stray bullet? An ambush while on patrol? And what useful purpose had been served by his death?

2

I closed my eyes, and when I opened them again I found that I was still standing in the hall of Sir William's house. This time, however, I was alone. Moreover, as I looked about me, I realized that, although I was in the same house, it was a house that had greatly altered. The light was no longer artificial and there was now no fire burning in the fireplace; the tiger skin and the heads of animals had been removed; there were different ornaments on the mantel-shelf, and, to the left, by the door of the room in which Sir William had been playing the guitar, there now hung on the wall a large portrait of him and of his wife. By their side, in the picture, stood the same small boy whom I had last seen saying good-bye to his brother; but in the portrait he was some years older, so that I now had no difficulty in recognizing that this boy was the young Sir Alfred Fothey who was still standing, I knew, with the other sightseers, attempting to produce some satisfactory explanation for my own death. For a moment I wondered by what trick or distortion of time it had come about that I was haunting this house, had haunted it indeed at a period which preceded my own birth. Then I opened the front door and stepped into the bright sunlight of a summer day.

Outside, too, the scene had changed. Most of the trees which I remembered had been cut down. In front of the house the drive had been widened, and on the yellow gravel several cars, of a rather antique design, were drawn up. Beyond them extended a spacious lawn which I had not noticed when I first came to the house; and at the farthest corner of the lawn, in the shade of some carefully trimmed tree, I could see chairs and a table, and a group of people sitting down. A maid was walking towards them across the lawn, carrying a tray on which the silver tea-pot and jugs glittered in the sun. To my right I heard the sound of voices and, looking in that direction, saw Sir Alfred Fothey, accompanied by a lady slightly younger than himself, walking towards me round the corner of the house past a bed of yellow wallflowers.

He was considerably younger than when I had first seen him. I should have guessed him now to be about forty-five years old. In his upright carriage and the firm set of his jaw beneath a bushy moustache, there was a dignity which verged on pomposity. He was evidently engaged in an argument with the lady at his side, who appeared to be pleading with him for some object which he was unwilling to concede. As the pair of them reached me, they both glanced towards the lawn and stopped still by mutual accord, as though wishing to finish their conversation in private. I stood close to them, on the steps overlooking the gravel and the flower-beds. It no longer surprised me that neither of them was aware of being overheard.

'But, Alfred,' the lady was saying, 'wouldn't it be possible even now, with the influence which you have, to get Harry transferred to some job at home?' She was a beautiful woman and looked up at him with large mild eyes in which the tears were standing. She spoke urgently, but not as though she expected her request to be granted.

Sir Alfred was swaying slightly on his heels. His hands were thrust deeply into the pockets of the white trousers which he was wearing. 'Perfectly possible, my dear,' he said, 'but I couldn't hear of it. No, the boy must take his chance, as the best young men in the country are doing. My father gave his eldest son. You know, my brother

Jack. You've often heard me speak of him. I couldn't bear to think that I'd failed in my duty.'

The lady looked down to the ground. 'He's our only son,' she said softly.

'All the more reason,' replied Sir Alfred, 'why we should set an example.' He paused, and patted his wife rather clumsily upon the shoulder. 'I know it's hard, my dear,' he said in a softer voice, and then, bracing his shoulders, he began to speak as though he were addressing a larger audience. 'But we've got to see this thing through, and to do that we must put our country first. Every time. Not ourselves, but our country.'

His wife spoke gently. 'I know, dear,' she said, and Sir Alfred smiled.

'That's the stuff,' he said more gaily. 'Besides, the boy himself wouldn't dream of any such idea. He's as keen as mustard.'

Lady Fothey was looking across the lawn towards the group of people in the shade. 'I sometimes wonder,' she said. 'It's not the same now after nearly four years as it was at the beginning. I don't know what it is. These casualty lists day after day. Sometimes one almost wonders whether it's worth while, whether it will ever end.'

'Good heavens!' said Sir Alfred. 'Worth while! Really! How would you like to see your daughter raped before your eyes? No. There must be no turning back now. We must give these fellows a lesson they won't forget in a hurry. After all, they started it.'

'Yes, I know,' said Lady Fothey. 'But it's always the innocent who suffer.'

Sir Alfred took her arm and began to walk with her

towards the lawn. 'Come, come, my dear,' he said. 'You mustn't be morbid. You really mustn't be morbid.'

I followed them across the lawn to the tea-table and the deck chairs. There were three people sitting in the chairs, a young man in the uniform of a second lieutenant, a girl of ten or eleven who was holding the young man's hand tightly between her own hands as she leant forward to him, and a rather older man in blue hospital uniform. His face was very pale and I noticed that he had lost one leg. His thin lips were pressed tightly together, and there was a strange, almost insane glitter in his restless eyes.

As Sir Alfred and his wife approached the young man had risen to his feet. He bore, I thought, a remarkable resemblance to the Hussar whom I had seen departing to another war; I noticed the same excitement and tenseness in his bearing, yet seemed to see in the eyes less elation and perhaps more thoughtfulness.

'Hullo, mother,' he said. 'Let me introduce Captain West. I met him in the village. He's just been allowed out of hospital, and was kind enough to come and have some tea with us.'

'Don't move, sir, don't move,' cried Sir Alfred as he saw the wounded soldier attempt to struggle up from his chair. 'Get all the rest you can. Very glad you're out of hospital. Not seriously wounded, I hope.' He had now walked up to the edge of the table and could see over the top of it that the Captain had lost one of his legs. He coughed in an embarrassed manner and was, I could see, about to apologize for his indiscretion. But Captain West spoke first.

'A mere scratch,' he said, 'thank you. A mere scratch.' His curiously cat-like eyes were fixed on Sir Alfred's face and his lips were still tightly compressed. From the tones of his voice you would have said that he was completely at his ease, yet in his face and in the tautness of every muscle there was sufficient evidence to the contrary. I, who had seen many others in a like case, could imagine the terror and exasperation which he felt whenever he moved one hand from the other's grip and saw the fingers quiver uncontrollably. I knew the effort of will which lay behind his most ordinary words, the restraint which he was setting always upon a mind which, without that restraint, would, he thought, whirl away into irresponsibility and inarticulateness.

Everyone was now seated at the tea-table. Lady Fothey had begun to pour out tea. I stood behind the chair in which the young man was sitting. Sir Alfred was opposite to me and Captain West a little to my right. I saw that the little girl was listening most intently to the conversation, staring meditatively, as a child will, now at the young man whom I imagined to be her brother, now at the wounded officer.

'It is a terrible thing,' said Sir Alfred, 'to think of the sacrifices which you fellows are making for us at home. The country must never forget it.' He paused, and in a soft gentle voice his wife echoed 'Never.'

A short laugh, like a bark, came from Captain West. He spilt some of the tea from the cup which he was holding tightly gripped on his knees. 'Not at all,' he said. 'We positively enjoy chucking away our arms and legs. We think how it's being appreciated at home.'

Sir Alfred appeared uncertain as to whether to take this remark as jest or earnest. The young man stretched out his legs in front of him and intervened in the conversation. 'Let's talk about something else,' he said. 'I expect Captain West has had about enough of the war for the time being.'

'Not at all,' said the Captain. 'Not at all, old boy. It's a fascinating subject. Absolutely unforgettable.'

'Ha!' said Sir Alfred proudly. 'I daresay you'd like to be back there again, taking another shot at the fellows.'

The wounded man looked at him sharply. 'Oh, absolutely, sir!' he replied. 'There are few sights which can compare with a row of entrails hanging along the wire.'

Here both Sir Alfred and Lady Fothey coughed demonstratively, indicating with their eyes the presence of a young girl. She, I noticed, had put her hand on the Captain's knee and was staring up into his face with large and interested eyes.

Lady Fothey rose to her feet. 'I think, dear,' she said, 'that it is time we went inside.' She beckoned to the little girl and pointed towards the house. 'Please excuse me, Captain West, and please don't move. I do hope we shall be seeing you again.'

The Captain raised the girl's hand to his lips. 'Don't mind me,' he said. 'You won't have fellows like me around when you grow up.' He attempted to smile, but his habitual compression of the lips caused his smile to appear more like a grimace.

The girl opened her mouth to reply to him, but, startled by his expression, withdrew without saying a word. After she had gone a few paces, she turned back.

'Will Harry come and say good-bye?' she asked, and Sir Alfred replied: 'Of course he will. You must give him a good send-off.'

There was silence for some moments while we followed with our eyes the two figures crossing the lawn upon which shadows had now begun to encroach. Then Sir Alfred cleared his throat and spoke again, addressing himself to the Captain.

'I expect Harry's told you,' he said, 'that he's off to the front to-morrow. You could probably give him a few tips. I daresay you've seen a lot of service.'

The Captain glanced quickly at the young man by his side. He nodded his head and began to speak, with his eyes still fixed on the shadowed lawn and the retreating figures.

'From the beginning,' he said. 'I volunteered on the second day of the show. I used to think that I was the hell of a hero. It may surprise you, but I used to think quite a lot in those days. My idea was that this war had suddenly put a lot of meaning into our lives. Before the war, I thought, our lives were being wasted, but now we had something to do with them. Actually there was quite a lot of chaps who thought like that. Well, don't do it. Don't think at all. That's all the advice I can give you. It's a waste of time and energy; and you can get along quite all right without thinking. If you don't think, the whole show is not without its amusing moments. You can even get some fun out of the actual fighting, picking the fellows off and mowing them down, and blowing them about, and all the time knowing that you won't be able to keep out of their way for ever. But once you start thinking, it spoils the whole show.

You begin to wonder what new meaning exactly you have got into your life, and what new meaning the brass hats are ever likely to put into it. You begin to wonder whether the enemy is as fed up with the whole show as you are, and what it's all about, anyway. Then you remember that it's something to do with "militarism," and it seems that there's a lot of that about. You think of home, but that seems to you funnier than all the rest. It really is. It's a perfect scream. All over the world you have the old men making money and the young men getting killed and the women running about between the two. It's what they call division of labour. We're the heroes, of course. We don't get the money; but we do see life. Oh yes. On the whole, it's not a bad war. It's the fellows who'll be in the next war that I don't envy.'

I saw that Sir Alfred was acutely embarrassed by the words to which he was listening. Indeed the atmosphere was a very different one from that which had prevailed in his father's house at the time when his elder brother was setting out upon his first campaign. His son, however, seemed more used to this type of conversation. He was leaning back in his chair with his legs extended and his hands behind his neck. From time to time he would glance at Captain West's eager, nervous face, and I observed that there was sympathy and kindness in his eyes.

Sir Alfred seized with relief upon the last point in Captain West's remarks. 'But surely,' he said, 'this is a war to end war.'

'Oh yes,' replied the Captain, 'so it is. I had forgotten. It seems to me such a funny way of going about it. That's all. But why end war, anyway? A lot of people like it. They'd feel quite lost without it.'

Harry Fothey spoke. He kept his eyes on Captain West's face and seemed anxious not to irritate him by an expression of too much seriousness, though he was unable to keep back what was in his mind. 'If it doesn't put an end to war,' he said, 'it will be just a crime. I mean I can't see how anybody will have any faith in governments or anything else if, after this, they're pushed into the same thing all over again.'

Almost as though I had made some move, he turned suddenly in his chair and, for a moment, seemed to be looking into my eyes. In spite of his youth and the nervous excitement which he felt there was a worried, anxious look on his face. He turned back quickly, almost with a startled air, to the table.

'Human nature, you know,' Sir Alfred was saying, 'takes a lot of getting over.'

Captain West was not listening to him. 'God!' he said, 'I'd like to see that next war. It'll break all records. Everyone will get a chance of seeing life. Civilians just as much as us. It'll be, "all in." Sort of "totalitarian," to coin a phrase.'

The young man spoke more urgently. 'No, no,' he said. 'We must stop it. When this show's over, we must see it doesn't happen again.'

Captain West had put his hand over his eyes. 'We?' he said. 'What's left of us.' His body fell back, not relaxed but twitching in his chair. 'Oh, God!' he said in a voice that was more like a whimper. 'What is left? What is left?'

I saw his shoulders heave with sobs, and it was some

seconds before he could pull himself together. Then he grasped his crutch and stumbled angrily to his feet.

'Beg pardon, all,' he said. 'I'm making a bloody exhibition of myself. I still have sort of attacks. Nerves, I suppose. Don't mind me. Good-bye, Sir Alfred. Thank you for the tea. No, don't come with me. I like being by myself. Good-bye, Fothey. Good luck! Cover yourself with glory. Cover yourself with glory.'

With surprising agility he stumbled off across the lawn, a weird figure like a lame and tropical bird that seemed out of place among the massive shadows and clean lines of carefully trimmed trees. Sir Alfred, in a state of extreme embarrassment, was still sitting in his chair. Harry Fothey had risen to his feet and was staring at the back of his departing guest. He took a pace or two forward as though to follow him and I moved also in his direction. I moved, not across the clipped grass, but into a quite different scene.

The last words of Captain West were still ringing in my ears: 'Cover yourself with glory. Cover yourself with glory'; and these words seemed unaccountably to blend into another sound, not of words at all, a sound which I knew well, the pounding of heavy guns in the distance and, closer at hand, the screaming and bursting of shells. I was standing on grey and slippery ground, in drenching rain. In front of me, moving forward, was still the figure of Harry Fothey; but now he held a revolver in his hand, and from time to time would look back to beckon forward those who were behind him. There were men in muddy uniforms to my left and right, and so familiar to me was the scene that for a moment I forgot my real condition and was dismayed to find that my hands did not grasp a rifle with bayonet fixed, as did the hands of the others.

The men were moving slowly and carefully, picking their way past broken segments of wire and the deep mouths of shell holes. Through the driving rain I could not see the position of the enemy's trenches, nor how much farther we should have to go before the charge. Suddenly the machine guns opened up on us and man after man went down crumpled, some to lie still, others to crawl slowly backwards to their own lines. I saw at once that we should never reach our objective; but the men still went forward.

In front of me Harry Fothey turned again, waved his revolver and shouted out words that were lost in the noise of shells and the stammering rattle of the machine guns. Men who caught his eye grinned. Their faces were tense and their eyes hard. They had been told, no doubt, while on training, that it takes 15,000 bullets to kill a man, and that the enemy, however expert in other ways, was unable to stand up to cold steel. They did not realize or appear to realize that their present position was hopeless.

I saw Harry Fothey turn once more, raise his hand above his head, and start to run forward. He had completed two or three steps when he flung both arms wide and fell sideways. His body slumped over the edge of a shell hole, and slipped down, head foremost into the grey and muddy water with which the hole was filled. Two men reached the same place and I saw them pulling at their officer's legs, attempting to raise him, but in the next moment they also had fallen, one on top of the dead body over the ugly lip of the shell hole, the other on his back, slithering over the slimy ground. I could see the legs of two men, the shoulders and elbows of one projecting from the water. I shut my eyes, and slowly the noise of battle died away. I could only hear the distant pounding of the heavy guns, the rustle of rain and a splash of water to which as an accompaniment still echoed in my ears the words: 'Cover yourself with glory. Cover yourself with glory.'

3

So these words repeated themselves in my head until I opened my eyes, and heard immediately a different voice, raised as if in expostulation and self-defence.

'But you don't understand. You don't understand.'

I was looking again at Sir Alfred Fothey and now there was little in his appearance to distinguish him from the man whom I had first met with the sightseers. He was seated in a comfortable arm-chair in front of a fire. At his back was a large writing desk upon which I noticed, in a silver frame, a photograph of his son wearing the uniform of a second lieutenant. In the photograph the boy looked gay and carefree, a different sight from what I had last seen of him.

There were tall windows in the wall away from the fireplace, and here, carefully arranging the folds of the black-out material which was behind the curtains, stood a young woman who, as she turned her head, immediately brought back to my memory the little girl whom I had seen sitting in the garden with her brother and Captain West. Through the window I could hear the noise of traffic, and so concluded that either we were in a different house or else that in the interval of years which had passed, some town with its busy roads had enfolded the place which I had seen before in the quiet country.

The young woman had drawn the curtains and turned back into the room. Her face was flushed, and there was an angry look in her eyes. I noticed that now she had grown to womanhood she bore a remarkable resemblance to her brother, although her face was more determined, perhaps, than his had been, and was certainly older. I should have guessed her to be a woman of about thirty.

Sir Alfred spoke again. 'Really, Mary, my dear,' he said, 'you don't understand at all.'

She sat down in a chair at the other side of the fireplace and looked across at her father. Her eyes were large and sympathetic, as her brother's had been. One lock of yellow hair hung low over her forehead, and below the lock of hair her gaze was level and direct.

'But is it true?' she asked. 'Is it true what that man was saying—that the company has been making all its money lately out of exporting aero-engines to——?'

Sir Alfred broke in. 'It's the laws of the market,' he said. 'Buying and selling. You don't understand. If we hadn't sold the stuff to the devils, someone else would. Now, look here, Mary, my dear. I admit I made a mistake. I just didn't believe it possible that those fellows would dare to have a crack at us. I was wrong—I admit it.'

She continued to look steadily at him. A slight constriction in the muscles of her mouth showed that she did not share or sympathize with his point of view.

Sir Alfred crossed one leg over the other and pulled a pipe from his pocket. It was evident that he was far

from feeling at his ease. After a pause he spoke again.
'Of course,' he said, 'you are too young to remember the
last war.'

She turned her head aside and looked towards the
window and towards me who was standing there. 'No,'
she said, 'I remember it well. I remember Harry going
out. I remember the lists of names read in churches,
and the prayers for the dead. I remember all the excitement we had at the armistice. I was at school then. I
remember reading in the papers of the people starving
and dying of disease all over Europe. We—I and my
friends—thought more about it than we knew we were
thinking at the time. One thing was obvious to us, that
never before had humanity sunk so low, never had the
religion to which we paid lip-service been shown so
inadequate or hypocritical. It was undeniable. There
was nothing to argue about. What more convincing
proof could there be of the rottenness of our world than
that mass-murder, the millions and millions of need-
lessly dead? What exactly was wrong and what exactly
needed changing, that was another matter. Was it our
attitude to politics, or economics, or religion or sex?
Probably all of them; here certainly there was room for
argument.

'On the main point, however, there was no room—
that our way of life, our way of thought had to change;
for it seemed to us monstrous to imagine that once again
the whole world could be plunged into slaughter. That
was what we thought, and we were right. But where did
we find among our leaders people who thought in the
same way, who saw the same urgency, who were able to
point to anything noble or encouraging? All we heard

were maunderings about "gradualism," cynicism about "the laws of the market," bluff about our inability even to feed those whom just recently we had described as unforgettable heroes. Now we shall feed them all right. Now we shall find that the "laws of the market" have miraculously disappeared. Now we shall be told that there is need for bold decisions. Why not before, when we could have used our energies for life instead of death?'

Sir Alfred was puffing at his pipe. 'No doubt,' he said, 'mistakes have been made. But recrimination about the past won't help us. We're all in this thing together and we must see it through. There must be no looking back until that gang of criminals has been destroyed.'

'Which gang of criminals?' said his daughter, and I could see that he was startled and shocked by the contemptuous bitterness of her voice. She also observed his dismay and the hard look in her eyes softened. 'Oh, I know it's unfair,' she said, 'to blame everything on a few people. We're all responsible. But still it's true that those who had the power and the wealth and the influence and couldn't use them, are the most guilty. What have they given us to fight for? Certainly not themselves. What have they left us? Only blind obstinacy and toughness and ordinary humanity. Everything else will have to be built up as we go along.'

Sir Alfred had not followed the latter part of her argument. 'Guilty!' he interjected. 'I don't know what you mean by "guilty." We didn't want the war.'

His daughter raised her head quickly. 'Yet perhaps they're using your engines,' she said. 'Perhaps their bombers were built with your money.'

'No, no,' he replied indignantly. 'A totally different type. Besides, we've been over all this before.' He was indignant, but I could see that he was deeply moved. He spoke again, in a strangely gentle voice. 'Good heavens, Mary, don't you think that I love my country?'

Then he stopped speaking abruptly, listening. From a distance, and then taking up the call from all directions came the wail of sirens, and with hardly an intermission the angry spasmodic cracks and rumbling of gunfire, and then the swelling drone of the engines of approaching aircraft. Sir Alfred was looking at his watch.

Mary looked towards him across the fireplace, and put one hand on his knee. She smiled. 'I'm sorry,' she said. 'I know you do. But is that enough?'

Her father rose to his feet, still staring at his watch. 'They're punctual to-night,' he said. 'Just time for a drink,' and he moved towards a cupboard in the wall to the left of the window. As he moved the noise of the aircraft seemed suddenly to increase and we heard the whistle of a bomb descending.

A crash, and a dull reverberation rocked the building. Mary ducked forward, with her head below the level of the table. 'Better get on the floor,' she said.

Sir Alfred remained standing by the cupboard. 'I'm damned if I get on the floor,' he replied. He stood erect, nervously beating the top of his head with his left hand. 'The devils,' he said, 'the devils, oh the devils!'

Next instant we heard another whistle and immediately afterwards there was a blinding flash, a crash much louder than before, a noise and a sensation like an express train sweeping through a narrow and crowded station. The light in the room went out, but not before

I had seen Mary fall forward under the table and Sir
Alfred crouch down, as I was doing, by the wall. There
was a sound of breaking glass, a rushing like the wind,
and then an uncanny silence, broken almost immediately by the high screaming of a woman in the street
below.

I rose to my feet. The black-out curtains and the
windows had gone. The room was illuminated by a dull
red light from outside. I could see now that we were
in a street of some large town, a different place altogether from the house that I knew. Sir Alfred and his
daughter scrambled to their feet. Both came to the
window and stood there at my side. We peered through
clouds of dust which slowly settled and revealed in the
distance four or five large and angry geranium glows
of flame. Nearer at hand a single house was burning
furiously, and the whole sky was filled with stars and
constellations of bursting shells.

'Lucky thing,' said Sir Alfred. 'The windows blew
outward.' He stared at the sight in front of him. 'Good
God!' he said. 'It's terrible. Women and children. It's
awful.' He paused for a moment and, in the flickering
red glow I could see his lips set grimly together. 'They'll
get it back,' he said. 'They'll get it back all right.'

His daughter had picked up an object from the floor.
It was the silver photograph frame containing the picture of her dead brother. She replaced it gently on the
writing desk.

'Yes,' she said slowly. 'Eye for eye, tooth for tooth,
man for man, city for city.'

The roar of gunfire, the distant explosion of bombs
seemed an accompaniment to her words. We continued

to look out at the night sky gashed with searchlights, punctured with the bursting stars of shells. Far beyond them glittered the real impassive constellations of the universe.

In the street below an ambulance had drawn up. From time to time we heard the high hysterical screaming of a woman from somewhere out of sight. Mary turned away, shrugging her shoulders. 'So it goes on,' she said. Then she touched her father's arm. 'I must be going. I'm on duty in ten minutes.'

Sir Alfred put his arm round her and kissed her. 'Look after yourself, my dear,' he said. 'Look after yourself.'

She opened a door into an adjoining room and in a moment or two returned wearing an overcoat and with a steel helmet in her hand. She waved gaily to her father from the door. 'Good-bye' she said. 'I shall be back soon. No ill-feeling, I hope.'

He kissed his hand to her. 'Of course not,' he replied, and as she went downstairs he continued to stare down upon the street. We saw her come out of the door and wave again to us and we followed her with our eyes to the corner of the street towards which she walked quickly, picking her way amongst debris and looking up from time to time at the sky which was quieter now, since the raid seemed to have shifted away from us or else to be fading out.

Sir Alfred turned towards me and said aloud, 'It's a difficult question.'

CHAPTER IV

The Rough and the Smooth

1

Sir ALFRED had hardly completed these words when I saw him again as I had seen him before, erect, with a puzzled expression, among the sightseers, and I was aware that all the scenes of his past life at which I had been present had flashed by in a second or the fraction of a second.

'This is a difficult subject,' he repeated, 'and I confess that I no longer think exactly as I did about it. War's a ghastly thing, I know. But that's no reason why we shouldn't be proud of our fighting services. Courage, loyalty, honour, interest in one's work—you can't get far without them.'

Again he paused and began to look about him in an embarrassed manner. It seemed that he was conscious that his words, in spite of the feeling that lay behind them, were obvious, banal and uninteresting. I myself, though I knew him better than I had done at first, though I saw that there was no insincerity in his pronouncements, nevertheless could not help observing that his state of mind was at least as perplexed as my own, and that all he had said or ever could say would be of little value in solving the question which I had put to myself.

I was surprised certainly at his inability to deal with this question, at the irresolution in his ideas which belied the strength and character of his face. We who were in the ranks had had nearly always the conviction that those who were in command of us were better acquainted than we with the objects of strategy and the final direction of our efforts. So I should have imagined that among civilians one who was greatly my superior in fortune, education, and influence would show also more understanding than I possessed. Yet he had said nothing which I did not know already. I was at least as well aware as he was of the value of those virtues which he had mentioned. I knew perfectly, and without the need for reflection, that I could depend at all times on my comrades-in-arms. We had been bound together not only by danger, but by loyalty and affection. I knew also of the interest and enthusiasm which many had in the actual work of fighting. I had seen mechanics handling their tanks as though these were the most cherished possessions that a man could have. I had known those who took as much delight in their skill with a bayonet as any cricketer could have in his ability to face the bowling. I had watched an elderly sergeant explaining to recruits the parts of a rifle; and he had seemed like an old gentleman proudly revealing his collection of birds' eggs.

All this was important; yet, for my present purpose, all this was beside the point. Certainly, our enthusiasms, our jokes, our conventions, the qualities which unified us were valuable; but before my mind's eye was still the picture of the countless dead in abject irresponsible positions, and together with that the extensive view and beauty which I had seen too late. I could not believe that anyone who had seen these two sights together and with the same clarity as I had seen them, could be permanently contented with the trifling accomplishments of fighting or even with that deep sense of fellowship which, however fine, was still a fellowship in monotony, danger and isolation.

Sir Alfred had arrived at a conclusion which had always been obvious to nearly all of us, namely that war was not a fine thing. He had seen off to their deaths, amongst others, his elder brother and his son. He had reverenced their memories and would no doubt have gone the same way as they had gone if he had deemed it to be his duty. Yet the value of these deaths was for him, as for me, something inexplicable; nor, it seemed, had he been seriously concerned to prevent their recurrence, in spite of the power and influence which, from his manner and the style of his life, he must evidently have possessed. I sympathized with him certainly much more fully than I had done at first sight, yet I had regretfully to admit that I could not look to him for any guidance whatsoever, since he was, on the main question, at least as ignorant as myself.

Was it possible, I wondered, that no explanation existed for my dilemma? Was the young man, Bob Clark, right in his assumption that I was wasting my time in this inquiry? Was war, and with it the death and maiming of body and mind, a fact of nature beyond

the control of individuals and hardly worth their discussion, incalculable and unavoidable like a rainstorm
or a fog?

I saw that the young man was beginning to speak.
'You've got to take the rough with the smooth,' he was
saying; but before he had finished his sentence I found
myself once more in different surroundings.

2

I was standing outside a large building of red brick
which was evidently a school. In front of me, through
two or three congested exits, boys and girls were stream-
ing out on to the black asphalt playground, jostling,
screaming, pushing each other, laughing, forming into
small groups or darting hither and thither over the hard
black ground. Behind my back a red winter sun was
setting and was now near the horizon, so that, as I stood
at the top of a short flight of steps overlooking the playground, my shadow seemed monstrously enlarged, cut-
ting right across the asphalt and the eager bodies and
faces of the children. The door nearest to me seemed
to be confined to the use of boys, and nearly all of those
who came out of it passed through or along my shadow.
Some of these would look up suddenly in my direction
almost as if they had been momentarily startled, but no
one showed me any sign of recognition.

For some time I listened to the children's excited
conversation, though nearly all of it was unintelligible
to me, since it consisted almost entirely of short sentences referring obliquely to the day's events, with eager
screams of approbation or dissent. It was a display of
life and energy, however unregulated, which came to

me almost as a shock after my recent experiences of adult life with the sightseers and in the family mansion of Sir Alfred. Here the quick gestures, the faces alight with excitement the unfettered ebullience of feeling, affected me strangely. For a moment I seemed unaccountably to have recaptured some of that sense of limitless space and of delicate absorbing detail which had come to me at the instant of my death. So I watched with sympathy the school children dispersing, as they crossed and recrossed my sombre shadow on the ground.

Soon they had nearly all gone through the large iron gates which separated the school playground from a main road, along which poured a stream of traffic— buses, heavy lorries and private cars, hooting, hurrying, noisy and dusty. Among the few children who remained on the playground I noticed one in particular, a boy of fourteen or fifteen, who was standing still at the very edge of my shadow and looked from time to time at the school building as though he were waiting for someone to emerge from it. His thin, peaked face was more serious and more diffident than it was when I had seen it before; yet it was easy to recognize in it the face of Mr. Bob Clark whom I had last heard replying to Sir Alfred. The boy, I could see, was nervous. He would continue to pull his cap down farther over his eyes and to finger the strap of the heavy satchel which hung upon his back.

I watched him closely and at length saw him straighten up, give a final tug to his cap and assume a more restful posture. I followed the direction of his eyes and saw a young man come running out of the school with a gown thrown loosely over one shoulder and a pile of books under his arm. His thick dark hair curled back from a

high forehead, and beneath the forehead the eyes were
vigorous and piercing. Everything about this young man
indicated an unusual energy and enthusiasm. But it
was not this overflowing vitality which immediately impressed and excited me.

What stirred my deepest feelings was the fact that I
knew this man already. He was Captain Wallace and
I had served in his company. Before the war he had
been, I knew, a schoolmaster. Now I saw him as he had
been and wished that I could see him as he was; for
he had been killed in action only a week or two before
me. How earnestly I wished to discuss with him the
questions which troubled me! To discover whether he
had seen what I had seen, whether he thought as I
thought, whether he could explain clearly and satisfactorily why we had both been killed! Even now in this
past time I desired to approach him, somehow to impress my presence on him, by touching him on the
arm, perhaps, or by shouting in his ear. I would explain
to him the events which would bring him and me
together, and find out in what light he viewed them.
Yet I restrained myself, for the project was certainly
absurd. I seemed to know that he would neither see
nor hear me. How could he recognize in me a part of
his own future, and a future, perhaps, in which he did
not believe at all?

He came running towards me and stopped still in my
shadow, grasping with one hand the shoulder of the
boy who was waiting for him.

'Sorry, Clark,' he said, 'very sorry to have kept you
waiting. Well, let's go right away. Your parents will be
at home, won't they?'

'Yes, sir,' replied the boy. 'They're expecting you.' He looked up and smiled at the master, but there was a reserve and a diffidence in his smile which rather surprised me. It seemed that he was by no means hopeful about the enterprise on which he and Wallace were engaged.

Wallace himself had not noticed the expression on the boy's face. He clapped him on the shoulder and said, 'Good, excellent, fine! We'll talk them round. You see. Now let's go.'

He set off at a great pace across the playground, gripping the boy by the elbow and laughing at some remark which he had made, but which I did not hear.

I did not catch them up until they had reached the main road and were waiting for an opportunity to cross the stream of traffic. While they were waiting Wallace had noticed a book under the boy's arm. 'What's this?' he said. 'Shelley? Good! Splendid! You must read lots of this. I used to know masses of it by heart once.'

We began to cross the road, dodging the buses and lorries. Wallace was declaiming.

> '*O wild west wind, thou breath of Autumn's being,*
> *Thou from whose unseen presence the leaves dead* . . .'

He paused as a motorist, putting on all his brakes, narrowly avoided us. 'Grand stuff!' he said. 'Perfectly terrific!' and we went on for a few moments in silence till we reached a long straight suburban street fringed with recently planted trees that appeared to be dying. Behind the trees were rows of small semi-detached villas, indistinguishable from each other, except by the names,

'GlenAlvis,' 'Peacehaven,' 'Burrowthorpe,' 'Craggy Crest' and others.

Wallace strode on vigorously, looking from side to side with apparent enthusiasm. 'I say, Clark,' he ejaculated, 'have you ever done any mountaineering?'

'No, sir,' said the boy. He too glanced round him. 'I've never been away from here, except once, when I went to my Auntie's.'

'I say,' said Wallace, 'that's a pity. Never mind. You must come with me some time to my hide-out in the mountains. It's marvellous. Miles from anywhere. We often have reading parties down there. It's jolly fine. Work all the morning and walk the rest of the day. There are heaps of peaks to climb. As a matter of fact what I like best is climbing by moonlight. I just can't stay in bed when there's a full moon. Must be out of doors. And I tell you what. Some of those mountain lakes at about three in the morning! Gosh, they're cold! By jove, that's the life, all right.'

I saw that a glint of enthusiasm had come into the boy's eyes while the schoolmaster was speaking. It quickly died away and he stared down mournfully at his boots.

We walked on for a time in silence and I observed that in the rows of houses people were beginning to draw the curtains in the front rooms, though some householders were still to be seen in the narrow gardens by their gates. They were fixing small pieces of stone in position to form crazy pavements or carefully surveying small beds of earth in which, at this season of the year, nothing was growing.

In a moment or two the boy coughed and spoke again,

nervously. 'Do you know what you're going to say to my father, sir?' he asked.

Wallace clapped him on the shoulder. 'Good boy!' he said. 'We must have a council of war, mustn't we?' He paused for a moment and then spoke in a graver voice. 'As a matter of fact I think it ought to be perfectly easy. It's absurd to think of your leaving school just when you're beginning to get somewhere. And if I can convince your people that you've got a reasonable chance of a university scholarship, I don't see how they can object. I mean, apart from anything else, it's a good investment.' He turned suddenly to the boy. 'Now tell me frankly,' he said, 'what you feel about it.'

'My dad's very determined,' the boy replied. 'He says you can't pick and choose.'

Wallace laughed and again clapped Bob Clark on the shoulder. 'Look here,' he said, 'I'm not interested in what your dad thinks. I want to know what *you* think. And, incidentally, the whole purpose of education is to enable you to pick and choose.'

The boy looked round him despairingly. By now we had entered a different street, narrower and more winding, but still with each house nearly indistinguishable from the next. 'Of course I'd like to stay on at school,' he began slowly, 'but . . .'

Wallace interrupted him at once. 'Good! Splendid! Terrific! That's all I wanted to know. We'll see to it all right. You just leave it to me.'

The boy seemed about to speak again, but, as he glanced up the road, he hesitated, then, after we had gone a few steps farther, said in a dull voice, 'We're nearly there now, sir.'

We stopped in front of a small house that was one of a row of four. 'Hopedene' was its name, and it was chiefly remarkable for a display in the narrow front garden of all kinds of dolls and cheap statuettes, which were arranged in groups on the grey and dirty soil as though they were holding some sort of a confabulation. I noticed effigies of the wolf and of little Red Riding Hood, of a mermaid, of Neptune, of a crusader amongst others. Some were stuck into the ground by their legs; others were attached to sticks; a few were leaning sideways in curious drunken postures.

Wallace stopped still in front of this collection. 'I say,' he exclaimed, 'what a jolly good idea! Is this what you do?'

The boy smiled somewhat shamefacedly. 'No, sir,' he said, 'My dad did all this. You know he's been out of work.'

Wallace was momentarily surprised. 'Jolly interesting, jolly interesting,' he muttered, and we made our way up the short path to the front door.

The room into which the boy showed us was small, and most of its space was taken up by a cheap wooden table in the centre. Between this table and the wall one had to edge one's way sideways if one wished to traverse the room. There were three or four chairs with their thin backs thrust against the rim of the table and their seats beneath it.

Opposite to us, as we entered, stood a tall thin man in his shirt sleeves and with his back to us. He was engaged in hammering a tintack into the wall, but when he heard our steps he turned round and laid down the hammer on the white coarse grain of the table. I noticed that his face was exceptionally white and sallow; beneath a drooping moustache his thin lips were pressed together, seeming to denote a kind of determination which appeared rather at variance with the expression of his weak and hesitating eyes. He spoke gloomily.

'Good evening. It's Mr. Wallace, isn't it? Take a chair,' and he himself scrambled into a chair between the table and the fireplace.

Wallace had advanced in order to shake hands, but was deterred by the difficulty of squeezing past two chairs and thus incommoding his host, who was already sitting down. He moved one chair back from the table, got astride it and pulled himself in. Bob Clark stood in a corner near the door, facing his father, and I stood next to him.

Wallace began to speak at once. 'Well, Mr. Clark,' he said, 'I expect Bob's told you why I wanted to come and see you.'

The other man nodded his head. I could see that he was looking at Wallace with a kind of suspicion of which Wallace himself was entirely unaware. 'I ought to say at once, Mr. Wallace,' he said, 'that it's no good.'

'Oh, come, come, Mr. Clark,' Wallace replied, slapping down one hand on the table. 'You mustn't condemn us unheard. This is a democratic country, you know. You must hear the evidence before you make up your mind.' He smiled confidently and engagingly, while Mr. Clark's face took on an expression of even greater gloom.

'That's all bunk,' he said, and, as he spoke, a woman, the boy's mother no doubt, entered the room from a door which faced me and which led, I could see, into the kitchen. She was drying her hands on an apron as she came in, and immediately attempted to shake hands with Wallace across a couple of chairs and her husband's back. Wallace tried to get to his feet, knocked his knee against some hidden portion of the table and sat down again.

'So good of you,' said Mrs. Clark in a very over-refined voice, 'so good of you, Mr. Wallace, to have called. You mustn't mind my husband's manners. It's being out of work so long that makes him a bit grumpy; but he isn't like that at all really. Oh no, I assure you, Mr. Wallace. I only wish you could have seen him when we were married. He was a bright young fellow then and no mistake. You'd hardly believe it, to look at him now. Isn't that right, dear?'

Mr. Clark looked up with some distaste at his wife's large and anxious face. He made no reply, being used, I imagined, rather to listen to her than to speak himself. Indeed on this occasion she hardly paused long enough to allow him to open his mouth.

'May I tempt you to a little tea, Mr. Wallace?' she asked and, without waiting for an answer, turned at once to her boy. 'Get Mr. Wallace a cup, sonny. You'll find the tea on the kitchen table. Don't forget the sugar. Get the blue cup with the yellow rim. Oh dear, what will Mr. Wallace think of me? He'll think I've only one cup!'

Wallace laughed and stopped the boy as he began to move rather reluctantly towards the kitchen. 'No thank you, Mrs. Clark,' he said. 'It's very good of you, but I'd rather talk. And I'd like Bob to be here while we're discussing his future. Now, look here——'

Mrs. Clark interrupted him: 'Just a weeny cup?'

The boy protested angrily. 'Mr. Wallace doesn't want any tea, mum.'

'Hold your tongue,' said Mr. Clark without making it clear to whom his remark was addressed, and his wife with some difficulty, since she was a big woman, edged her way in to the table and sat down, leaning her massive face on her hands. She looked sideways at Wallace in an attitude of attention, but almost immediately spoke again.

'It would be lovely to have Bob at college,' she said. 'I'd be ever so proud; but his dad's terribly set against it, and we need the money, no mistake.'

'Mr. Wallace was going to say something,' said her husband slowly, and Wallace looked at him gratefully. He spoke quickly, to avoid further interruption, and in a businesslike manner. From time to time he glanced towards the door where the boy and I were standing, as though seeking from this quarter a sympathy that was not forthcoming elsewhere.

'It's like this,' he said. 'I can guarantee—I hate using the word, but I really think I can guarantee—that if Bob stays on at school he will get a university scholarship in two or at most three years. Now I know that will mean some sacrifice from you, but my point is that putting it on the very lowest level—the financial level—it's worth it. He'll obviously get a better job when he leaves the university than he's likely to get now. But that's the least of the advantages, I think. The thing is that he's got a good brain and he ought to be allowed to use it. Why, there's masses of stuff he's just getting on to and which he'll enjoy no end. It'll be hard work, but he'll revel in it. It'll be marvellous, won't it, Bob? Terrific fun.'

He paused, the least bit embarrassed since no one appeared to be in the slightest degree infected by his enthusiasm. The boy himself was looking nervously at his father who stared at the table in front of him with an expression of distaste upon his face. Mrs. Clark had, I think, ceased to listen after the first two or three sentences.

Wallace spoke again, somewhat sententiously. 'I want you to put the boy's interests first,' he said.

Mr. Clark raised his head and licked his lips. He looked gloomily at the boy and then all round the table. He was, I could see, a man who as a rule spoke little but, on being moved to speech, made this an occasion of some solemnity. He coughed and settled himself in his chair before opening his mouth.

'I want you to get me quite straight, Mr. Wallace,' he said. Wallace leant forward attentively and nodded his head. The other continued: 'First of all, of course it's the boy I'm thinking about. I won't say we can't do with the extra money. Of course we can. But it's the boy himself we put first.'

He sighed and then turned suddenly to Wallace with a strangely ferocious expression on his face. 'Now, sir,' he said, 'I want to ask you a straight question. Where does all this education lead? No, don't answer me now. Let me finish. I'll tell you. It doesn't lead anywhere.' He raised his hand in an awkward but effective gesture of authority to check Wallace's interruption. 'Being out of work,' he continued, 'for eighteen months, I've had a lot of time to think things over and I've reached my conclusions.

'Now take *my* case. I was all through the war till the armistice and after. Took a long time getting demobbed. Longer than seemed right; but really that was the best part. Then I came back here. We'd read in the papers that we were heroes, but by the time we got back people had forgotten about that. There was a bit of work at first. Not much, but enough. Then what? Nothing at all. And I'm a skilled worker. Now all this makes you think. Who's running all this? Who's on all the boards and committees? Who's in the government? Now we're coming to it. It's the people who've had this higher education you talk about. You'll pardon me, Mr. Wallace, if I say that it doesn't need much education to see that they're no bloody good. Why, even in the army we could always find a job of work for men to do. But these fellows can't, not until there's another war. And they won't be long before they have one, the way things are going.'

Wallace could no longer be restrained. 'I see your point,' he burst in excitedly, 'I see your point exactly. But surely that's an argument for more education, not less.' He paused triumphantly and then, seeing that Mr. Clark was not in the least impressed by his reply, he continued in a more thoughtful voice. 'I agree that things have been badly managed; but you've got to remember that we live in an age of transition. Post-war problems aren't easy. It's a slow process adapting ourselves to changed conditions.'

Mr. Clark went on as though he had not heard the schoolmaster. 'That's point number one,' he said. 'The educated classes aren't getting us anywhere. And never will, by what I can figure out. I remember in my dad's time everyone was saying that education would cure everything. Once get the working class educated, we used to say, and there'll be a change. Well, look at things to-day. Those who've risen up out of the working class are no different to the rest. They're worse.

'And another thing. There was a Captain I knew during the last war. He was a gentleman and he'd been to the university. Captain West he was called, a funny sort of chap, I used to think, but lately I've begun to see that he talked sense. I can remember him saying to me, "Clark," he used to say, "when that kid of yours grows up" (I'd told him we had a boy) "when he grows up, see that he doesn't read too many books. They'll give him the wrong ideas, because life isn't like what you read about in books. Look at me, Clark," he'd say. "When I was at college I never read about these bloody lice and these rats. I learnt about a language called ancient Greek. And what we want is more mechanics, not a lot of damned amateurs like me." That's what he used to say. He was shot about pretty badly in the end. And that brings me to point number two, which is where the boy comes in.

'Now I read the papers a good deal these days and I know that they don't tell the truth. But if you've got time to look at them carefully and read between the lines, then you get a pretty fair idea of what's happening. And I'm very much mistaken if things aren't working up to another war which is going to be bigger than the last one. Now mind you, I don't say who's going to fight who. It's too early to tell; but I say there's going to be a war and it won't be long. Three or four years perhaps. No more. Now what's going to be the effect of that? First of all there'll be plenty of work for all, and good wages too. And who's going to benefit most? At one end of the scale there'll be the big profiteers, and at the other end will be the skilled workers, particularly the young ones, those who are getting their training about now.

'Well, then, now we come to it. The boy's got a real chance at this new aircraft factory. He's not going to be turned off when he gets old enough for a man's wage. Why? Because they'll need him. I reckon by the time the next war starts he'll be sitting very pretty. He won't be called up and he'll be getting good money. So that's my answer to you, Mr. Wallace. The boy'll do a great deal better by going the way I want him to go than by messing about at school filling his head with a lot of stuff that doesn't work. That's flat.'

He stopped speaking and leant back in his chair, evidently satisfied that his arguments were unanswerable.

His wife turned towards Wallace in a conciliatory manner. 'He speaks rough,' she said, 'but, believe me, Mr. Wallace, he means what he says. To look at him you wouldn't think he was so determined, would you? That's from being out of work so long. Really he's a man that knows his own mind, and I think he's right too, though with no disrespect for you, Mr. Wallace. We think you've been very kind. And it would be

lovely to have the boy at college, wouldn't it, sonny?'
She glanced up at Bob Clark, who had been following
his father's speech with great attention, and now looked
with a rather quizzical expression on his face at the
schoolmaster.

Wallace was frowning and tapping the top of the
table with his knuckles. I had seen him often later at
the front in this very attitude and could hardly restrain
myself from attempting in some way to make my presence known to him. Soon he looked up and began to
speak quickly and incisively in a manner that I well
knew.

'There are two points in your argument, Mr. Clark,'
he said. 'First, that education has proved itself to be
inefficient. Second, that another war is likely to break
out in a few years. The first point I won't deal with,
because I'm sure that a little reflection will show you
that you're mistaken. Mistakes most certainly have been
made, but it's only with fuller knowledge and more good
will (and that's what education means) that we'll be
able to rectify them. As for the second point I beg you
to take my word for it that there'll be no war. I've been
a student of history myself all my life and I've got
friends abroad who really have inside information. It
just couldn't happen. No one could afford it. It's an
economic impossibility. We may not have learnt much,
but we have learnt that from last time.'

He looked eagerly at Mr. Clark and then, seeing no
sign that his remarks had taken any effect, he turned
his eye to the door where I was standing as though he
were likely to receive assent from there.

Mr. Clark had not moved a muscle of his face since he had concluded his speech. He had remained staring in front of him, and now, when he spoke, he did not look at Wallace. His words were slow and curiously emphatic.

'I've said my say, and you've said yours. It's a waste of time going on with this, because I fancy I'm right and you fancy you are. Maybe we're both wrong. Time will show. And now I'm going out.'

He rose from the table, nodded to Wallace and made his way through the door leading into the kitchen.

Mrs. Clark also rose hurriedly, pushing, as she did so, the table and Wallace with it back against the wall. 'You must forgive him running away like that, Mr. Wallace,' she said. 'Really you must. It's his evening at the club, and he was never one for an argument.'

Wallace had succeeded with some difficulty in scrambling towards the door. He spoke nervously and with a strange note of despondence in his voice. 'But is there nothing I can do, Mrs. Clark? I should be terribly sorry —worse than that, it would be a crying shame—if Bob doesn't go on with his education. He'll never have the chance again.'

The woman looked at him in evident surprise at the emotion in his voice. 'Well, well, Mr. Wallace,' she said, 'I suppose we all think our own job's the most important, and there's really no knowing, is there? But speaking for myself I really think that the boy is going to do quite nicely, and a great help that will be to us. And I don't think that you or I could talk his father round. He's an obstinate man, Mr. Wallace, and getting more so, though you might not think it to look at him.'

'You've not asked the boy what he thinks,' said Wallace, and the woman smiled broadly.

'Why, he wouldn't know,' she said. 'He's not had our experience.' She edged her way towards Bob and ruffled his hair with one of her large hands. Wallace looked closely at him, wishing evidently to extract from him some profession of disagreement with his parents' attitude; but the boy looked merely embarrassed.

'I'm not sure either, sir,' he said to the schoolmaster. 'Anyway perhaps it's better to do what my dad wants. And I'd be earning a wage from the start.' He looked at his mother, answering her smile.

Wallace sighed and went to the door. 'We must talk more about it,' he said. 'Definitely we must have another consultation.'

Then he said good-bye and went out into the dark street, almost touching me with his arm as he squeezed past the table.

I noticed that during Wallace's departure the boy had dropped on to the floor the book which he had been carrying under his arm. He paused for a second as though about to pick it up, then stepped over it towards the fireplace and began to straighten his tie in front of a small mirror that hung over the mantelpiece.

His mother sighed in relief. 'There,' she said briskly, 'that's that.' She added in a softer voice, 'He means well, I daresay.'

The boy continued to stare in the mirror. He was surveying himself keenly, as though this was his first acquaintance with his own face.

'When do I start, mum?' he said, without turning round; but I did not hear his mother's reply.

3

Instead of any words I heard immediately the roar, rattle and scraping of machinery. I was in an enormous room and was looking again at the boy who indeed was now a boy no longer, but scarcely younger than he had been when I first met him. He was one among many others bent over the machines, and at his side, wearing a white coat, was an older man who appeared to be giving him instructions. I could see the lips of the two move, but, since I was standing some yards away from them, I could not hear the words which they uttered above the din and clatter of machinery which filled **the air.**

The young man's face seemed paler than it was when I saw him last, although this may have been the effect of the brilliant lighting which came from a source behind my back and threw sharply and distinctly against the white wall which faced me the shadows of the heads and shoulders of men, while over, beneath and around these shadows I could see whirl, drive and rotate the running and plunging images of pieces of machinery in a ghostly disorganized and unrhythmical dance. A great bar or piston of blackness seemed to drive itself deeper and deeper into the shadow of the young man's head. His hands were moving quickly and deftly over the work with which he was occupied, and the shadows of his hands fluttered uneasily like butterflies against the hard unyielding background.

Somewhere in the high roof of the building a bell rang, and the machines swung to a standstill. It seemed at first as though a complete silence had supervened. At most the sound made by the men's feet and voices was a shuffle and twitter of ghosts after the powerful procession of the movement and noise of the machines. I certainly regarded them with respect, for I could imagine the contribution which they made unrelentingly to the mass of the material of destruction, and beside them the men, for the moment at least, appeared feeble and ignorant.

Soon my ears grew accustomed to the different sound of human conversation, which had replaced the whir and grinding of metal. Most of the conversation was concerned with technical details of the machinery. The workers, I could see, were conscious of their skill and proud of it, though none of them, I imagined, had any clear idea of where and how the machines upon which they were occupied would finally be employed. I heard one voice raised above the rest:

'The hours are long, but the money is good.'

And now the workers began to leave the building, with Bob Clark, in whom I was chiefly interested, one of the last to go. Behind them, at some distance, I followed past the motionless shadows on the wall. By the time I reached the door there was only my own shadow that moved among them, so that for a moment it seemed to me that I alone was alive and that the real bodies of men who had preceded me were the insubstantial creations of my mind, less solid than the dead lumps of metal which still appeared silhouetted on the wall to mark my own movement.

I followed the young man to the factory gates and out into the road where it was difficult to pick one's way among bicycles, buses, tramcars and the crowds of departing workers, men and women, boys and girls. Bob

Clark was now wearing a light grey suit of clothes. The trousers were carefully pressed, and from the corner of his breast pocket protruded a triangular strip of purple silk. I went with him across the road and saw waiting on the other side a figure who was already familiar to me. It was the girl whom I had seen hanging on the young man's arm among the sightseers: now she was staring into the windows of a book shop. Bob Clark, coming up to her, slapped her gently on the behind and she, when she saw him, smiled.

'Look at all those books,' she said.

Her companion followed her eyes to the display inside the window. 'Too many of them,' he said, 'by a long chalk. Not that there isn't money in books, if you write the right sort. But most of these writers don't get as much as I do.'

The girl looked at him proudly. He continued: 'Now there's a fellow'—he pointed towards an edition of Shelley—'there's a fellow who would have made a packet, only he died too soon. Give me the cash down every time.'

'That's poetry,' said the girl and then, looking at her watch, she turned away from the shop. 'We must hurry,' she said, 'or we'll be late.'

They turned together and began to walk fast away from me while I followed through the crowds of people, all hurrying, all apparently oppressed by some sense of urgency, glancing from time to time at their watches, or at the protruding faces of clocks which stood out like monuments from the high windows of the houses between which we went.

Soon we left the crowd and stepped aside into the wide vestibule of a cinema. No one observed my presence as we passed from the bright light into the dim interior of the building and took our places standing at the back rows of comfortably padded fauteuils, since there was no further seating accommodation. We turned our eyes to the screen on which was depicted the elegantly dressed figure of a woman descending an enormous marble staircase to the notes of a minuet by Beethoven.

As she went from step to step a hush, broken by an occasional sigh, fell upon the audience. The young woman at my side gripped her friend's hand convulsively. 'Lovely, isn't it?' she whispered, and he nodded his head, retaining her hand in his while keeping his eyes fixed upon the screen.

By this time the photograph of the lady had reached the bottom of the stairway. The music ceased as she turned sharply to her left, and advanced towards towering double doors which were immediately thrown open to her by tall servants in evening dress, who evidently were stationed there for that very purpose. On the threshold she paused to survey a room much vaster even than the hall through which she had just come, and indeed remarkable in every way.

In the very centre was a long dining-table, brilliant with glass and silver, and, as the door opened, men and women could be seen, in long robes and exquisitely tailored outfits, rising from their places and turning with full wine glasses extended in their hands. One of them pronounced the word 'Victory,' but the spectator's attention was inevitably distracted from these ladies and gentlemen by the singular furniture of their dining-room, one wall of which was entirely taken up with rows of books in glass cases, while the other wall consisted of long tanks of water in which were swimming backwards and forwards, slowly circling or poised still in their element, the various bodies of marine creatures—conger-eels, hermit crabs, sperlet, sea-horses and anemones. And the very end of the room was open to the air. Through this aperture, and over the heads of the diners who were still standing, unanimously extending their wine glasses, one could see the swaying branches of palm trees and half the circle of the moon rising far in the distance over an expanse of ocean. Slowly across the opening walked the graceful but absurd figure of a giraffe, and for a moment his large and peaceful gaze seemed to meet mine above the heads of the actors on the screen and the crowded figures below me that nestled together sighing in the warm seats.

'Some people know how to live,' the girl at my side whispered, and again Bob Clark nodded his head.

'That's the life all right,' he said. 'A bit far-fetched though.'

I had turned my eyes away from the screen and was peering at the backs of heads below me. Some were drooping forward in apparent sleep, others rested on shoulders or together, like coconuts propped against each other. To me, my mind full of recent impressions—the crowded streets, the relentless march of machines—these photographs of a lady and of a giraffe seemed oddly unreal and almost uninteresting, yet I could see in those of the spectators who were nearest to me something devout in the concentration of their eyes and in the fixity of their faces.

The music crashed into a final chord, and the heads below me altered their relative positions. There was a hum of conversation, and here and there I saw the flutter of handkerchiefs and the glint of glass or metal, as women dabbed their eyes or paid attention to their lips. It was evident that the big moment of the entertainment had passed, for, during the news reel which followed there was a continual fidgeting; the heads jerked from side to to side; comments were no longer uttered in a whisper.

Yet to me the scenes now in front of us were more interesting than what had preceded them; for we were watching a procession of troops and I did not need the aid of captions in order to recognize the army to which they belonged. I saw that they were moving over a frontier to take up positions from which some years later I and others would attempt to dislodge them, and I watched closely the order of their march, their faces and details of their equipment. There were one or two members of the audience who hissed and a few who clapped, but the majority appeared wholly uninterested by what was before their eyes, although many of them, as I had the best of reasons for knowing, would themselves before long become deeply implicated in the movement photographed in front of us.

There followed some scenes taken by cameramen in a remote part of the world where heavy fighting was at this time in progress. It was a war which certainly did not seem to the audience connected, as it was, with the much greater war that would presently engulf them all and kill many of them. Indeed the shots which now passed across the screen appeared to the majority rather amusing than otherwise: a roar of laughter greeted one scene of actual fighting in which a soldier ground his rifle butt into the face of a prostrate enemy. But I, who had seen such sights before and suffered from such actions, could not find them laughable.

I began to wonder how it could possibly happen that this audience of my fellow-countrymen could ever recognize me or the urgency of my question; for they were wholly incapable of understanding what was occurring before their eyes, while I was invisible. But I reflected that I was now with company who were alive before my death, that I myself at this past time which I had now re-entered, had formed part of such an audience as this, and that at the real time in which I existed, if I could be said to exist, there might be different people with a different way of looking at things.

I turned back to my companions and heard the girl whisper to Bob Clark. 'Always war. I'm fed up with it. Why can't we have something nice?'

'What do you call nice?' he asked, grinning at her, and she leant towards him, resting her head on his shoulder.

'You know,' she said, and there paused for a moment or two. 'And nice clothes . . .'

I looked away, but my eyes immediately found the pair of them again, and in a different scene.

4

However, almost before my eyes caught sight of them, my ears were full of a familiar sound, the wail of sirens, swelling from the distance, one after another, until the air was full of their rocking cries. I looked about me and saw that I was in a small sitting-room which had evidently been recently furnished. Red roses on the new carpet flared upwards to the pink silk of a lamp shade. New curtains of emerald green were drawn across the windows so meticulously that the folds on one side seemed to be matched exactly by those on the other. Two low arm-chairs, with rather narrow backs, upholstered in silver oil-cloth, were drawn up in front of a small fire, and between the chairs was a small table on which a china cupid upheld an ashtray of gun-metal.

The girl, who by this time might be, for all I knew, Bob Clark's wife, was sitting in one of these chairs. I was by the window and she had turned her head towards me when she heard the sound of the sirens. Bob Clark was leaning over the chair in which she sat, and he too had raised his head quickly and was looking in my direction. In a moment he straightened his back and thrust his hands into his trouser pockets.

'Lucky it's my night off,' he said. He began to pace backwards and forwards across the small room, and, there being no reply to his remark, he added, 'Funny sort of honeymoon this, and no mistake!'

The girl turned her head towards him and smiled. 'Makes you feel quite creepy, doesn't it?' she said.

He laughed. 'I don't know about creepy. What I'm thinking about is the furniture. I wouldn't like to lose that. We'd get precious little compensation till after the war, and then probably there wouldn't be the stuff to buy.'

'There's us too,' said his wife, and he replied, 'That goes without saying.'

Again he looked quickly towards me, for we could now hear the sound of gunfire in the distance. 'As a matter of fact,' he said, 'we've got some good stuff coming along now. Not enough of it yet; but before long we'll be able to let them have it all right.'

The girl by the fire shuddered slightly. She was straining her ears to hear the very distant drone of the engines of aircraft. 'I know it sounds silly,' she said, 'but I wish you weren't making those things. I wish you were making something else.'

He spoke sarcastically. 'What would you like me to make? Mud pies? I'd get paid a fat lot for that!'

She was still serious. 'No,' she said. 'I wish you were making something nice. Like furniture.'

Bob Clark walked towards her and patted her on the cheek. 'Listen, May,' he said. 'The work I do is skilled work. As for what we make in the factory, that's no business of mine, is it? You can't pick and choose. Come to think of it, I didn't start the war either.'

His wife leaned her head forwards on her hands, and stared into the fire. 'I'm sick of the war,' she said. 'You know there's a lot been killed already.'

'Mustn't be unpatriotic,' said Bob Clark. 'The war's on, and I suppose it'll go on till someone wins. There isn't anything we can do about it. We must just do our best.'

'You're not in the army, anyway,' she said, and she

turned her eyes towards the place where I was standing. 'I suppose we must be thankful for small mercies.'

There was a pause of complete silence. Bob Clark nodded his head towards the window. 'Looks as though they're not coming our way to-night,' he said, and added, as he rested his hand on the top of his head, 'touching wood.'

His wife sighed and settled back in her chair, but as the tension passed from her face, so did its vivacity. Her cheeks appeared somehow loose and flabby, and there was a dullness in her eyes which I had not noticed previously.

Bob Clark had evidently received the same impression as I had. 'Why don't you put something on your face?' he said as he seated himself in the other arm-chair. 'I like to see a woman who's got some life about her.'

His wife continued to stare into the fire. 'Listen, Bob,' she said. 'There's something I've been meaning to ask you. Couldn't we have a baby? It would be so nice.'

Bob Clark sat up quickly in his chair as though he had been suddenly stung. 'Good God,' he said, 'who put that idea into your head?'

The girl spoke with what was evidently an artificial and somehow desperate animation. 'I was round seeing Mrs. Humphreys this morning,' she said. 'She's expecting, and she seems ever so pleased.'

'Well,' he replied, 'she won't get to the pictures again for some time.' He spoke lightly, but it was clear that he was greatly agitated by his wife's proposal.

She continued to speak slowly. 'There is that of course,' she said, 'but I don't think I'd mind so very much, and it wouldn't be at once either. But I don't see what's so wrong with having a baby. It seems sort of natural, somehow.'

Bob Clark began to speak angrily. 'Natural?' he said. 'And there's nothing natural about not being able to pay the rent either, I suppose. Now look here, girl, we've got ourselves fairly comfortable' (and here he cast an appraising glance round the room). 'Don't let's go and spoil it all. I want a woman who looks desirable, and doesn't keep me waiting. I don't want to be messed up with children and things. Let's have a good time first, anyway. Let's have a bit of peace and quiet.'

The girl remained slumped up on her chair in front of the fire. There was a petulant frown on her face, and at the moment there seemed to me little in her appearance that could provoke physical desire. 'Well,' she said, 'if you say so, I suppose that's it. But where's the peace and quiet anyway? It's all right for you; but all I seem to do is shopping and the pictures twice a week. I sometimes think that somehow there ought to be more in life than that, and I thought perhaps a baby would help.'

'Now, look here,' said her husband severely, 'you're getting what they call neurotic. I used to have ideas like that once myself. I used to read poetry and things, Shelley, for instance.'

'I know you're very clever,' said the girl, 'but I don't see what Shelley's got to do with babies.'

Bob Clark spoke vigorously. 'It's not exactly that, but it's all the same sort of thing. I mean talking about "life" and what there is in it, or what there isn't, or what there ought to be. We don't know any of these things, and it's a waste of time bothering about them.

We don't even know why this war's on, let alone anything about life. The thing is to know what one wants and to stick to it. And I've told you what I want. I want a decent wage, which I'm getting, and I want a wife who is a wife and who's glad to see me when I get back home.'

'But I am,' said the girl tearfully. 'I'm terribly glad to see you. That's why I want to have a baby.'

'And I tell you,' said Bob Clark, 'that it would ruin everything. Good lord! In the middle of a war, too. You must be crazy.'

'Sometimes I think,' said his wife, 'that the more people there are being killed the more one ought to have babies.'

Her husband interrupted her. ' "Ought?" there's no "ought" about it. You're just nervy, that's what's wrong with you. Why, no one has kids these days. Not if they've got any sense. Later on, maybe. Things may alter. But at present it's just mad. I wouldn't mind betting that ninety per cent. are accidents.'

There was a short interval of silence which was broken by the swelling chant of the sirens sounding the 'All clear.' Bob Clark immediately sprang to his feet as though he had suddenly been released from some constraint. He rubbed his hands together and took up again the position which he had held previously behind his wife's chair. 'There,' he said, 'cheer up, old girl. They're not coming here to-night. Let's see what's on the radio.' And he turned a knob in a set that rested on the floor by his wife's chair.

His wife remained in her position, staring into the fire. With the tips of her fingers she was rubbing the skin which covered the lower portion of her eyes. In a moment a different voice rang out in the room. The voice was old and tired, but the enunciation was remarkably clear.

'To my mind,' said the voice, 'our greatness as a nation consists chiefly in this—in the fact that each one of us is able and anxious to take a purview of the wider issues of policy.' The voice coughed, and then continued: 'There has come into existence to-day a union of all nations and all creeds, a union indissoluble except by what is unthinkable—defeat. Together we march forwards towards a newer and in many ways a brighter world; nor will we lightly sheathe our sword until we have attained those aims for which in the first place that sword was unscabbarded.'

At this point Bob Clark switched off the wireless. 'Put a sock in it, chum,' he said. And then, turning to his wife: 'Bet your life that's one of the fellows who landed us in this jam. The world's all right, if only they'd leave us alone. But it's either war or babies, by what I can see. One thing is—you *can* stop having babies.'

His wife had let her head fall forward on her hands. I could see her shoulders heaving and a line of tears trickling down the powder on her cheek. 'I wish I knew what to think,' she said. 'I don't understand anything.'

Bob Clark spoke authoritatively. 'Don't be soft,' he said. 'Don't think. Why should you? It doesn't pay. Thinking won't alter things. You've got a nice house, haven't you? We're not doing too badly, are we?'

She shuddered slightly and looked up, past the furniture, to the ceiling of the room as though it were the roof of a trap. 'I can't help it,' she said. 'There must be something more.'

Her husband began to pat her on the back. 'Steady does it,' he was saying, 'steady does it. Don't run away with yourself. Maybe it's only something to do with the time of the month.'

She continued to stare upwards at the ceiling and took no notice of his hand which stroked the purple wool of the jumper which she was wearing.

As I watched her it seemed to me that her eyes were endeavouring to pierce through the plaster and wood-work that lay between them and the view of the night. I could have told her what she would see if she could see as I did—a vast vault of blackness studded, in the incredibly remote distance, with the flickering light of gigantic and incalculably numerous worlds. It was a sight, which, in my lifetime, I had viewed without a tremor, but now it filled me with conflicting feelings, sometimes with a strange dismay, sometimes with exultation, sometimes, when I forgot for a moment the question which troubled me, with a profound sense of peace. Yet it would not be of this immensity or those far luminaries that she would be thinking. Her mind no doubt would be set on those small but important portions of sky which this moment were being traversed by bombing aircraft whose loads would find out people like her and like her husband in one country or in another. She was not gifted, it seemed, with great powers of independent thought. Her mind was at least as per-plexed as my own and, in the end, she would no doubt take her husband's opinions for granted. Yet in her fear and her frustration there was something infinitely pathetic, so that I was shocked when I heard again her husband's voice, as he stroked her shoulder.

'You've got to take the rough with the smooth.'

CHAPTER V

The New Order

1

As HE spoke I saw him again with the group of people who, together with the priest, were arguing about my death. His wife was clinging to his arm, as I had seen her before, and was gazing up at him as though in admiration of what he had said or was about to say.

I knew at once that neither he nor she could provide an answer to my question which would be in the least degree satisfactory; yet, as I reflected upon their past which I had seen, I was struck by a curious similarity between them and Sir Alfred Fothey. Neither Sir Alfred nor they, it seemed, had ever considered the world in which they were living except from a point of view which had been laid down for them once and for all in the period of childhood. And this, although, until quite recently, Sir Alfred had been wholly convinced of the certainty of his opinions, while Bob Clark no doubt considered himself a person of unusual intellectual powers which he was capable of applying realistically to any situation which might confront him.

None of these people had intended any harm to anyone, yet the harm had come to themselves, to their children, to me and to many others; and they were wholly at a loss to explain it.

Neither of those into whose past I had now entered was even capable of feeling what a soldier must feel, since in each case accident of one kind or another had prevented them from approaching the fighting front, though now and to a certain extent the front had come to them.

That I should have died for Sir Alfred's notion of honour, or for Bob Clark's furniture seemed to me somehow ludicrous, and, in the second case, perhaps particularly so; for it seemed that, if Bob Clark had his way, the human race would before long become extinct.

I looked from face to face among the sightseers and my eyes were arrested by the appearance of that elderly man with a foreign accent whom I had guessed to be a scholar. In his face was an expression which he shared with none of the others; it was a kind of dumb and animal suffering, with terror also there, and a resignation which was somehow the strangest and most hopeless thing of all. When he spoke his eyes flashed and there was a great sincerity in the tones of his voice; but all the animation which he gave to his words seemed a mere epiphenomenon, something different from, and, though perhaps of a higher quality, less solid and fixed than the depth of dumb endurance that seemed to well up and support his frail body. He looked apologetically at the priest before he spoke. 'But there is evil,' he said. 'I must honour whoever resists it. If he is ignorant, never mind. If he is wise, by that the better.' He paused, and looked directly at me. 'I know,' he continued, 'from my own people, from my son.'

He was staring into my eyes with a strange intensity, so that I lost sight of the others and found myself again in a different time and place.

2

I was in a comfortably furnished sitting-room and at my first glance over the furniture and the bookcases it occurred to me that there was something unfamiliar about the style and arrangement of chairs and tables, as also about the bindings and titles of the books, so that I guessed that I was in some country other than my own. I was standing by the window and, as I turned to look through it, I saw all round me the high white walls of blocks of buildings, avenues of trees, an expanse of city, with cars thronging the streets and, in the distance, the glint of blue water, a lake, perhaps, or the sea.

I turned back to the room and observed that in it the bookcases were perhaps the most conspicuous articles of furniture. They were filled with books in many languages and, from a quick inspection of their titles, I received the impression that, while much space was devoted to the general literature and philosophy of most European countries, there was a predominance of books on medicine and science.

At a high chair by the window, close to my side, was sitting a woman with white hair. Her small and delicately featured face was a strong one and there was something both bold and restrained in the uprightness of her posture and the quick precise movements of her hands which were busied with a piece of sewing.

I heard the slightest sound outside the door of the room and saw this lady immediately lay down the sewing on her lap and turn her head sharply to the door. She sat more rigidly than ever.

By the fireplace, in a large well-covered arm-chair, was sitting the old scholar, or refugee, whom I had seen before and whom I guessed to be this woman's husband. He looked younger than he was when I had last seen him, and there was a grimness, perhaps a more resolute expression, about his mouth. He had been reading a book, but now he set the book down on the arm of his chair and looked up, in a curious attitude of alertness, at the door of the apartment. I could not help being surprised at the strangeness of the contrast between the apparent comfort of the room and the nervous anticipation of its occupants.

There was a gentle double knock on the door, and the man and the woman looked quickly at each other, with evident relief. Then the old scholar went to the door and opened it, ushering into the room another man of about his own age, well dressed and with a heavy walking-stick in his hand. And while this newcomer was exchanging the ordinary civilities with the lady of the house I was surprised again; for her husband was occupying himself in carefully locking the door and, when this was done to his satisfaction, he came toward me, so close that I had to move aside while he shut the window and, although there was plenty of light from outside, after switching on one of the reading lamps, drew the curtains. It appeared almost that this was the centre of some conspiracy; and yet the men and the woman were most unlike conspirators. To me they seemed people whose appearance and manners were attractive, interesting and inoffensive.

The visitor had now seated himself in a chair facing the old lady. He still held the walking-stick in his hands, and I saw from the expression on his rounded egg-shaped face that he was somewhat at a loss for words. He passed one hand over his thin hair, sighed, and stared downwards at his well-polished shoes. There was a look of great kindness and also of weariness in his eyes. At last he raised his head and began to speak, looking directly at the old lady.

'I am most deeply sorry,' he said. 'I have heard a little of the story about your son.' Suddenly he leant forward and pressed her hand, while she looked gravely at him. Then he turned his eyes aside, so that he was facing me, spread his hands apart in a gesture of weariness and despair, and exclaimed, 'Where will this end?'

The old lady also turned her head towards me. 'It will end in hatred,' she said in a low voice, 'and death and starvation and war.'

There was a long pause until she spoke again. She was looking at no one in particular and seemed almost to be speaking to herself.

'When I think of the last war,' she said, 'I cannot help thinking of an old woman whom I used to visit. Her son had been reported missing, and she could do noth-ing but sit indoors in her chair, rocking herself to and fro. "My boy," she'd say, "where is my boy?" and noth-ing we could say to her was any good. In the end she died. That kind of thing is very terrible.'

She stopped speaking and looked down to the floor, pursing her lips together. It seemed that she had spoken almost involuntarily and now wished to recall her words.

The visitor put his hand before his mouth and coughed. He looked enquiringly towards her husband who now began to speak. I pitied him since it was evident that a strong emotion made it difficult for him to control his words and the tones of his voice. He attempted to speak calmly and objectively, but this attempt was the more pathetic since from time to time his voice would break and he would have to pause, and his jaws would move as though he were biting something, before he could resume what he intended to be a straightforward and almost ordinary narrative.

'It was this morning,' he said. 'You know it is the day for his final examination. He would have done well. Very well. Of that there is no doubt. I should know since I have prepared him. He was not allowed to take the examination. Neither he nor others. Forty or fifty of them. All those who were suspected themselves, or whose parents were suspected, or who were not of the right blood. They do not want such people for doctors, they said. They will want doctors enough before long.'

He looked at his friend and sighed. Though his words were indignant, there was little indignation or bitterness in his voice. Soon he spoke again.

'They dragged these candidates outside the university. It was a case of young men taking the law into their hands, or it was made to appear so. In fact there is no doubt that these people were acting under orders. Most of the students they beat, tormented, insulted and released; but our son resisted; he said, it seems, what he thought, what we think, of the régime, and now we do not know where he is. A concentration camp, of course.

But I am afraid. He is brave and outspoken and intelligent. It is a combination of qualities that is not desired.'

He stopped speaking and, as he looked across the room at the others, his face expressed both sorrow and bewilderment. His friend was tapping the wood of his walking-stick with the fingers of his right hand, while with his left he made the stick gently rotate. There was a look of strain in his eyes and again he seemed at a loss for words. I thought that there was something terrible in the resignation of his posture and in the quiet voice which I had just heard. These men seemed to me like sentient things that know themselves ineluctably held and clasped in the workings of some vast regardless machine. They looked curiously at the doors and windows, and at length the visitor spoke again.

'Naturally,' he said, 'you have no idea where they have taken him.'

The father and mother glanced into each other's eyes. 'No,' said the scholar, 'one can guess. That is all.'

For a moment or two there was silence. The old lady had laid down her sewing on her lap and was staring at a photograph on the mantelpiece. I followed the direction of her eyes and saw the face of a boy of perhaps sixteen years old. I noticed his bright eyes, light curly hair and pleasant smile. It was a happy face, I considered, carefree and somewhat irresponsible.

'What I fear,' said the old lady suddenly, 'is for his spirit. They are clever, and his character is not yet formed. He is a little wild. He is a little doubtful. He has not known security, as we knew it when we were young.'

The two men looked at each other. There was both doubt and despondency in their eyes. The father of the boy sat up suddenly in his chair. He slapped his knee with his hand and, as he spoke, his eyes flashed.

'Ah, no!' he said; and there was something like agony in his voice. 'It is impossible.' He looked rapidly round, almost with a startled expression, at the rows of volumes in his bookcases, as though they had something to do with the present situation. He seemed about to add something to his words, but checked himself and, resting his chin on his hands, contemplated, as his wife was doing, the photograph on the mantelpiece.

The visitor moistened his lips and began to speak, turning now to the mother and now to the father.

'I personally,' he said, 'cannot believe it. Anyway we must hope. What is terrible is that there are grains of truth mixed in with their poison. But the poison is stronger than anything. They are making a new species. Perhaps later on those whom they have drugged will wake up; but then it will be too late.'

He paused and looked towards the window where I was standing. Then he too turned his eyes to the photograph at which the others were looking.

3

And as I also fixed my eyes on the boy's face I found that I was no longer in the sitting-room, but in a large and almost unfurnished wooden shed. I was standing at one end of the building and in front of me on the floor of unstained wooden boards were arranged rows of benches on which were sitting, motionless and silent, forty or fifty boys and young men. Directly before me, at the end of the first row, I recognized the boy whose photograph I had been looking at a moment previously.

He, like all the others, was dressed in what seemed to be the uniform of either a prison or a school—a grey shirt, and grey trousers, and thick black boots.

I saw that these people were listening to some sort of a lecture or exhortation. At my side was the speaker, a young man, though rather older than the majority of his audience. He was wearing a semi-military uniform and a revolver was slung on his belt. His face was remarkably intelligent, though there was a certain stiffness and over-confidence in his bearing which prevented him from being, to me at least, attractive. He spoke calmly and precisely and I observed that he was certainly retaining the attention of the youths in front of him.

I watched in particular the boy whose photograph I had just seen and I saw that the boy's face was grimmer than it had been at the time when he was photographed. He was listening intently to the lecture and, as he listened, he would sometimes nod his head as though in agreement, and sometimes he would appear puzzled and rub the back of his hand across his eyes.

'We have picked you out,' the speaker was saying, 'from all the rest in the camp for three reasons. Firstly, because you are of the same blood as we are, and we believe that those of the same blood should be blood-brothers. Secondly, because we think that you have got into trouble not so much by your own fault as by the fault of your parents or teachers who have shown an irresponsible and selfish attitude in their dealings with you. Thirdly, because it is our policy to give everyone the chance of sharing the opportunities of greatness, of loyalty, and of happy service which we are providing for the whole people.'

I observed that there was a strange and almost mystical assurance in the speaker's words and attitude. It was an assurance which could hardly help communicating itself to his hearers. He paused for a moment and looked round confidently, almost sympathetically, at his audience before continuing.

'What I want first,' he said, 'is for you to understand. I want you to know what our true aims are. Then you can judge for yourselves, without any constraint, whether or not they are nobler and more practical than the ideals which have been put before you in the past by sentimentalists and by hypocrites.

'Just consider for a moment your parents and your teachers, and not what they say so much as what they do. Ask yourself what it is to which they attach most value. You will agree, I think, that in most cases it is physical comfort or the enjoyment of some rather ridiculous kind of prestige. The minor functionary considers himself at least superior to a postman, and derives enormous self-satisfaction from this opinion of himself. The man who has a more expensive suit of clothes or a larger house than his neighbour is convinced thereby of his superiority. There is a whole hierarchy of individual self-importance, and words such as "success" and "independence" are used in congratulation of those who have managed to cut themselves off almost entirely from the lives of their fellow-men.

'Now consider the religious and moral ideas of these self-seekers, these liberals, democrats and rationalists. They are not quite so absurd as they would appear at first sight. For although it may seem fantastic that these people should speak of the brotherhood of man, of

international good will, of universal tolerance, of ideas
that transcend the boundaries of nations—in point of
fact this type of faith suits their book very admirably.
Even financiers and bishops have some moral sense, and
it is conceivable that they might feel some shame for
their complete indifference to the poverty and lack of
purpose of their own people, if they could not manage
to convince themselves that their far-reaching ideas for
world-brotherhood were of enormous value to their
friends, the Eskimos, or their brothers, the head-hunters
of New Guinea. What is characteristic of these idealists
is extraordinary selfishness in their private lives and
complete abstraction in their ideas which are, in point
of fact, meaningless. You may consider money as a symbol for both sides of their natures. In definite sums it is
kept in private hands and used for every purpose of
luxury and self-aggrandizement. In its total operation
it is blind, meaningless, abstract from real life, international in the sense that, though it spreads everywhere,
it is nowhere controlled for the particular good of any
single people. This is the ghostly, but powerful, apparatus which our individualists have prepared for us,
and through its operation working people have lost, or
are losing, everything which in the past made life fine
and noble—love of country, comradeship, purpose, self-
sacrifice, pride, chastity and honour.

'But we who are young have the right and the duty
to restore these qualities to the life of our nation. We
cannot bear the meaningless abstractions, the general
benevolence of which is hypocritical and serves only to
cut us off from our comrades, men and women, of our
own blood. We will not tolerate the tyranny of money

over flesh and blood. We do not propose to wait until the Eskimos become affiliated to the international banks. What we want is here and now—a world fit for our own people to live in fully.'

The speaker paused and looked down eagerly at his audience. It was evident that his words had not been ineffective. Some of the youths in front of him were staring at him with admiration in their flashing eyes; others appeared puzzled, as though a wholly new point of view were being put before them. Only a few, I thought, were entirely hostile to what they had heard. And now the speaker adopted a more intimate manner. He leaned forward slightly and, as he did so, brushed back from his forehead a lock of hair which had fallen forward during the speaking of his last agitated words. His voice was lower, as he continued.

'We are accused,' he said, 'of savagery and brutality. Many of you, I know, are here against your will. I want to speak quite frankly on this subject. These are the facts. We know that we are working for the good of every man, woman and child in our great country. On that point there can be no argument, only explanation. Now, this being true, it is necessary for us to achieve our aims as quickly as possible. Why should the hopes and ideals of the young wait interminably from disillusioned generation to generation for their fulfilment. We know that we shall encounter opposition. On every side we are confronted with stupidity and bad faith. This fact we accept frankly and we deal with it honestly. We will beat down opposition with the sword, and we will secure our own rights with the sword. It is a cleaner and nobler weapon than the nets of hypocritical diplo macy, or the creeping strangulation of international finance. But never will we refuse to our own blood-brothers an opportunity of turning their backs on an inglorious past and of entering with us the real paradise of our national future.'

Again he paused and stood for a moment stiffly at attention. Whether or not this was the conclusion of his speech I did not know, for I had heard enough and now went out through the door of the shed into the open air. Before I left I looked closely at the face of the boy whose photograph I had seen in his parents' sitting-room. There was little doubt that he had been profoundly moved by the words which he had heard. As he gazed up into the speaker's eyes there was a fixed smile upon his face. His eyes were narrowed and there was a determination about the chin which had not been evident in the photograph.

As I looked at him I reflected that there was little doubt as to where in the end he would be found. It was possible that he would, owing to the compulsion of what he conceived to be a grand ideal, betray his father and his friends. Certainly he would be in one of those detachments of picked troops of which I had had experience on several battle-fronts, expert fighters and wholly convinced, at least at the beginning, of the justice of their cause. In some ways we used to admire them for this, though on the whole we did not like them. And, as I thought along these lines, I began somehow to lose interest in the boy, not caring much to know whether now he was as I was, or whether he had survived.

4

I left the room and found myself in an open and treeless expanse of sand. At a little distance in front of me there extended what seemed to be an endless wall of wire, and, at intervals of twenty or thirty yards to right and left of me I observed the stiff marching figures of sentries and their fixed bayonets. They were performing their patrol with an almost uncanny regularity and precision; indeed there was something almost ludicrous in the sight of so many men, widely spread out as they were, marching in step for a short distance, halting together, coming to attention, as far as the eye could see, turning, and repeating exactly the same procedure, first to the right, then to the left, interminably, with the stiff rhythm of automata, so that I might have thought that this great enclosure with its guardians was some absurdly exaggerated plaything or mechanical toy, did I not suspect that it was a structure designed for anything but amusement.

So, for what seemed to me a long time, I walked along the wall of wire past indistinguishable sentries, some of whom looked up suddenly at me as I went by, though none recognized my presence. From time to time I passed various groups of men and women engaged, under supervision, in invariably mechanical activity. Some, with sentries to watch them, were digging holes in the ground; and what was most odd in this performance was the fact that every movement of each digger was exactly synchronized with the movement of his neighbour. The words of command would ring out, and at each word fifty or more men would do precisely the same action, whether it was to drive the spade into the ground, to fling the sandy earth on heaps two paces to the rear and left of each body, or to pause for perhaps a second with straightened back, not, however, with much relief from labour, since each man's eyes were fixed continually upon the commanding officer.

As I looked along the rows of faces I could see that they were of all types and of many nationalities. There were some faces which were dull and brutish; others with noble features from which the vitality had been drained; faces old and young and middle-aged, in which there could be no natural uniformity, yet upon which had been imposed a terrifying sameness through the direction of the eyes in fear to an unchallenged supervisor.

I watched the precisely regulated motions of unnecessary labour continue, and for a moment it was almost a relief to the eye when one of the diggers, an old man, fell forward across his spade and remained lying on his face, sprawling over the half-dug hole. Immediately the others stopped digging and stood for a short space of time in attitudes which differed slightly each from each; even when they started again on their labour, the rhythm had gone; meanwhile the officials were bustling hither and thither and some of them were blowing whistles.

The whole scene reminded me of what happens when the outer wall of a termitary receives some sudden blow, an event for which no calculations have been made. There is a short period of unrest and convulsion. The heart of the machine misses a beat in an intense dismay. And so for some minutes I saw the organization of the labour squad disrupted, until there arrived from some

other quarter of the huge enclosure a fresh group of
officials who had been summoned by the whistles of
their fellows. Two of these newcomers attempted to
raise the old man to his feet, but I could see clearly,
as he struggled weakly, that his knees were not strong
enough to support his body. Then, as he sank back
again into the hole in the sand and began to cover his
face with his hands, one of the officials drew a revolver
from his belt, pressed it into the old man's side and
fired one or two shots. And soon the body was covered
over with earth; the diggers resumed their work, with
a uniformity almost as precise as before, though from
time to time one or another would steal a glance sideways to the humped ground where one of their number
was lying inactive; and all these, I reflected, men and
women (for I could see women also on the barren
ground, marching and counter-marching in prison uniforms and with close-cropped hair, performing under
the eyes of instructors physical exercises with dumb-
bells or with Indian clubs)—all these are the natives of
many countries who have been forcibly subjected to an
idea of life which is wholly foreign to them. They have
been taken from their homes and families, and so been
cut clean away from every natural prejudice, piety or
affection. In their new mode of life they are not for
one moment allowed to consider themselves as human
beings, as creatures with horizons which are, as I know
now, enormous and perhaps illimitable, with prospects
of fascinating complexity and of simple delight. Instead
friend is cut away from friend and the eye is made to
serve the revolver or the whip. The very muscles of the
body are forced to respond to a rhythm which is im-

posed from elsewhere. I knew that there could be no
end under the sun so lofty as to justify the employment
of such means towards its attainment.

So I thought; and my horror at what was before my
eyes made me unwilling to return again to the shed in
which the eager minds of young men were being forced
to a kind of ideal brutishness. As I have said, I was no
longer much interested in the fate of the old scholar's
son. He had begun to seem to me scarcely human, a
creature infected hopelessly, violent, in spite of his
arrogant ideals, and not to be cured except by the
violence which he would himself invoke. Even the look
of him in the photograph, his eager and boyish face,
aroused in me too little sympathy; and I closed my eyes,
expecting to open them again in the religious building
near the circle of sightseers.

5

Yet, as my eyes were closed, I began to think, as one
often does on these occasions, quickly and intensely,
with a revulsion from the feelings I had had when I
was looking about me at the actual scenes of the concentration camp. I began to see again in memory the
kindly bewildered features of the man with the egg-
shaped head who had called to offer his condolences to
the scholar and his wife after their son's arrest, and
who had twiddled the walking-stick between the palms
of his hands as he spoke dubiously of the future. I
thought too of the old lady, the boy's mother, of the
pride and integrity which had been evident in her whole
bearing; of the old scholar himself and of his carefully
selected library. These, I knew well, were not the people

to produce monsters. These had no wish to kill or to be killed. They would be, I imagined, as unable as I was myself satisfactorily to answer the question which never ceased to trouble me. Moreover it was not only they who had failed to give to their children an assurance and confidence in life sufficient to make them believe it to be as valuable as in reality I knew that it was.

Sir Alfred Fothey had not been able to put before his children anything more inspiring for their guidance than a kind of conventional loyalty to what existed, and this quality had, in his case, been fostered in an atmosphere of wealth and leisure. His daughter, it seemed to me, had been justly critical of his attitude. Bob Clark's father had fought in one war and then been left with nothing better to do before the next than arrange small statuettes in his meagre plot of ground. It was not surprising that he could recommend to his son nothing finer than the certainty of a job and some immunity from danger. And, though he and Sir Alfred differed so widely in character and upbringing, and put before their children such opposed ideals, yet they had, it seemed to me, this in common—that each was oppressed by a sort of despair, a willingness to accept what was wholly inacceptable, something of cowardice which made them most uninspiring to those who were younger than themselves. They offered no adventure and their inactivity was unsupported by any show of wisdom.

Was it not to be expected, I thought, that young men who had grown up in such an atmosphere would be deeply affected by such slogans as I had heard from the propagandist in the concentration camp? 'We will not

tolerate the tyranny of money over flesh and blood'
they were told; and it was not necessarily an ungenerous
sentiment that responded to such an appeal. Youth, I
knew, was most difficult and dangerous. Its horizons
were enormous and so was its zest for exploration. It
was easily impatient of those professedly experienced
guides whose instructions tended rather towards limit-
ing than encouraging ambition. Yet for all its ardour
and impetuosity, for all its diffused and extended vision,
it still deeply craved for discipline and direction. For
without these the eye becomes in the end something
indistinguishable, terrible or unknown.

It was easy then to see how the young converts in the
concentration camp would accept with enthusiasm what
would seem to them a far-reaching and a worthy aim;
and, having done so, they would welcome the strict discipline that was required for its attainment. They would
look with contempt upon such a one as Bob Clark, a
man whose whole life, they would say, was founded on
fear and insecurity; whose work was purposeless, whose
love was sterile, whose pride was concerned with nothing more valuable than furniture, handkerchiefs, entertainment at the cinema.

As for Sir Alfred, he would seem to them both gross
and irresponsible. They would regard his patriotism as
pretence, since he was willing to dispose of the instruments of war for money and without thought of how
or when they would be employed. Indeed they would be
able to see no purpose in his life except the acquisition
of wealth and the conventional employment of it.

They would feel themselves infinitely superior to

such persons, and to me also who even now had no clear idea of why precisely I had been killed. Yet however enviable was their enthusiasm or their self-confidence it remained true that neither Sir Alfred nor Bob Clark would willingly co-operate in such an action as I had just seen, when an old man was murdered for no better reason than that he was too weak to stand up.

I began to see that the self-conscious direction of the will to a certain aim is not necessarily a quality to be admired, that to hesitate and to doubt may be more human than to believe and to assent. Yet even here my mind could not rest, for still it had found no assurance except of its own ignorance, nor was there anything more admirable in the qualities of indecision and insincerity because I had found examples of evil in their opposites.

I opened my eyes again upon the group of sightseers and looked for a moment or two half-expectantly from face to face, as though I could trace there some evidence that they too were affected by my own dilemma.

The old scholar was still speaking. 'My son,' he said, 'whom I taught myself, he gave evidence against me to the police. It was not through him. It was the evil idea. He believed he was right, but he was not right. The general death must prove that.'

I saw that the man with the mackintosh was looking at him grimly.

'That is just what we are discussing,' he said. 'The "general death," as you call it, what does it prove? That there are criminals, certainly. But what and where are they precisely? At one time what seemed right to me seemed easy and obvious. It still seems obvious, but there are even more enemies than I suspected.'

He paused, and as he did so both his face changed and his surroundings.

CHAPTER VI

The Man from Spain

1

I WAS in a small room by a table which was covered with books. The curtains of the one window were drawn and the light from beneath a red shade shone on old-fashioned ornaments, dogs and pigs in china, small bronze goddesses, and upon pictures of wide-eyed stags or cows, furniture that contrasted somehow with the piles of books which were, I noticed, mostly concerned with philosophy or politics, so that I was led to believe that I was in a lodging-house and that the two young men who sat before the fire, with their feet extended and with pipes in their mouths, were members of some university.

In one of them I had no difficulty in recognizing the man in the mackintosh who had just spoken to the old scholar. He was much younger, indeed a boy of no more than seventeen or eighteen years old, and there was much less severity and determination about his face than there had been when I last saw him. There was more animation, however, I noticed, as he leaned forward in his chair and looked enquiringly at his companion, having apparently reached the end of a sentence which he regarded as important.

I followed his eyes and saw that the other man was the elder of the two by several years. His appearance was tidier and his manner more restrained. I would have guessed him to be a young fellow of a college or a senior member of the university. Now he looked sympathetically at the young man, and began to speak, smiling as he did so.

'Charles,' he said, 'you may think me cynical, but I can assure you that I've met many people who've been exactly in your state, and they've all grown out of it. It's a phase through which nearly all intelligent people go. I've known it myself. I remember once deciding that I'd have, for my peace of mind, to do one of three things— either join the Catholic Church, or the Communist party, or get married. Well, look at me now. And I believe that there are other alternatives to-day.'

Charles smiled quickly, but almost indulgently. Then he frowned as he continued speaking. 'Perhaps you were right then,' he said. 'Perhaps it's a fact that we only get one or two chances in our lives of exercising free will, and that, for most of us, these chances come in our youth. It might have been better for you to have become an active communist, or to have got married deliberately as a way of living, even to have become a priest, though I doubt that. What I mean is that you would have consciously chosen your whole scheme of life, instead of just taking it as it comes along, and being shaped by it, whether you like it or not.'

His friend interrupted. 'And perhaps I should have made a complete ass of myself. Perhaps it's true that, even with my excellent results in examinations, I'm not quite competent enough to know what is the best way to live, and that it's a better plan to wait and see and perhaps grow wiser than to plunge into some extreme or other and either live to regret it or else stick on through pride and end up in a psychologist's case book.'

Charles was knocking out his pipe against the iron fender. I noticed the tension of his hands, indeed of his whole face, and knew that this argument was for him serious. He was trying, I could see, honestly to weigh up what was true in his friend's words and at the same time to control the impatience which he felt when he found his own ideas treated lightly or contradicted. He continued to look down into the fender, and spoke somewhat bitterly.

'You've got a way of making everything I say sound priggish. You'd probably talk like that to Socrates.'

'I probably would,' replied the other, 'but the question doesn't arise, because you're not Socrates.'

Charles threw back his head and laughed. He looked across at his friend and there was something, I thought, most engagingly open in his face, as he acknowledged the rebuff. 'No, I'm not,' he said, 'and you're quite right to tell me so.' He paused and again his face took on an expression of severity. 'But even then,' he continued, 'you're not really right. People ought to imitate Socrates in their small ways.'

'I do my best,' replied his friend. 'He was an adept at suspending judgment.'

Charles slapped the arm of his chair with his open hand.

'No he wasn't,' he said. 'That's just where you're

wrong. That's just where you make everything great somehow littler so that it will suit your book. What did Socrates say? That the whole of life should be spent in training for wisdom, and by wisdom he didn't mean examinations, but learning how to live justly. I know you can twist that about too. You can say that he was never dogmatic, that he required a great deal of curious metaphysical research before he could pretend to know anything. But that's not the real truth, that's just an excuse for our own inactivity. And when you talk about "suspending the judgment" what you really mean is "be irresolute, leave the injustice and poverty and war in which we live for others to deal with, be comfortable, be infinitely tolerant of everything that doesn't directly affect yourself, pour cold water on generous enthusiasms that seem to you likely to disturb what you've always known." That's what you really mean.'

He had spoken fiercely, but now, as he looked across at his friend and saw that, though his words had had no very pronounced effect, he was regarding him sympathetically and with affection, he suddenly smiled again, as though in apology for having expressed himself too forcibly.

'But I believe this,' he continued, and then rose suddenly to his feet and picked up an open book from the table. 'Listen,' he said. 'I was reading this just now.' He began to read aloud and I could see that, though he read soberly enough, the words which he read were moving him strangely. 'Man's dearest possession is Life, and since it is given to him to live but once, he must so live as to feel no torturing regrets for years without purpose, so live that, dying, he can say: "All my life and all my strength were given to the finest cause in the world—the liberation of mankind." '

I too, as in my situation I was bound to do, had found these words moving, and I looked with sympathy at the young man, as he laid down the book on the table and said gravely 'That's Lenin.'

His friend shifted somewhat uncomfortably in his chair. He took the pipe from his lips and put it down upon his knees before he spoke. 'A bit pompous,' he said, 'thought I suppose that's a quality which is inevitable in any pronouncement about Life with a capital L.' He observed a look of disappointment in his friend's face and went on speaking quickly. 'Don't think I'm unsympathetic, Charles. But it just isn't quite so easy as all that. I forgive you your hasty skipping from Socrates to Lenin, apparently without a thought of how these two great men would have disapproved of each other. But it's really there that the trouble lies. There are plenty of fine sentiments; the difficulty is when it comes to applying them to real life. What, for instance, is the precise meaning of "the finest cause in the world, the liberation of mankind"? To Lenin presumably it means the expropriation of the expropriators, whoever they are. To a Christian it would mean a regeneration of the heart. To Socrates it would mean right thinking. To a Buddhist it would mean a cessation of desire. All fine ideas, no doubt, but all in the end ruined by practice, as no doubt Lenin's will be before long, even if they are not already.

'After all, what religion has gone in so thoroughly for persecution as Christianity, the doctrine of which, to an outsider, would appear peculiarly averse from burnings and tortures? It will be just the same with Leninism, which is also a religion in its own way. At first it will be all "The People," the long-suffering people with its sane and healthy instincts opposed to the sefishness, perversion and decadence of "the ruling class"; just as, perhaps, in the dawn of Christianity, though Roman soldiers were everywhere visible, men's minds were pervaded with a peaceful and limpid atmosphere of a loving God. But before long there will be schismatics. It will be found that "the people" are not always sane and healthy, any more than the universe is always, or indeed often, kindly. There will be rival factions, each determined that while its own theory is "the finest cause in the world" that of its opponents must be stamped out as heresy. There will be, of necessity, a new "ruling class" and it will remain so however much it may be called "the people," since "the people" *en masse* have never yet shown any desire or ability to rule themselves. The real "people" will have to be dragooned, no doubt for their own good, and a number of vexed questions will arise as to how many wrongs make a right.

'I am not saying that very great improvements in the standard of living may not be brought about by Lenin's methods, or indeed by many other methods. All I object to is the dignifying of political change by the title "the liberation of mankind." It's a tall order.'

He looked quizzically at Charles who had been following his words closely and now burst in, speaking with a kind of indignation. 'You're so nearly right,' he said, 'that you are completely wrong. Things continue to exist however much you pick them to pieces. It is you, not I, who are romantic and revivalistic, or rather you're not, but those are the qualities on which you base your argument. Because a thing isn't perfect in a moment, you reject it entirely. Because you can't conceive of man as wholly liberated, like God, you are content to leave him with all his chains. Suppose all your forecasts are correct, what then? I maintain that something irrevocable and tremendous has been achieved already, a necessary stage precisely in what we are talking of, the liberation of mankind. Attack this, if you like. Prove that men are more free under a system of irresponsible private ownership than they are under a socialist system. Then your argument would be worth answering. You might be right and I wrong. It is a thing that hasn't yet been put to the test. But don't pour cold water on every fine idea simply because, as we both know, men are not saints and often make mistakes. Your argument is dishonest. You're only dealing with the outsides of things, or their parts taken separately. And then you laugh at what isn't whole and complete. It's an easy game, but it's not thinking.'

He paused, as though for breath, and his friend smiling, said 'I fancy we are becoming emotional.'

Charles, however, remained looking fiercely and indignantly at the elder man who sighed, as though he would gladly leave the discussion here, then leaned forward and began to speak more incisively than he had done before.

'Tell me of something,' he said, 'which is whole and complete. In the old days it was Perfect Being, or God, something which very few people pretended to understand, but to which as an ultimate standard the incompleteness and partiality of the world was referred. You don't believe in God. I again suspend my judgment. But I don't talk glibly, as you do, of wholeness and completeness. I don't know what they are. And I doubt very much whether you do either. I don't think you would, if you thought at all about it, put up a mere system of economics as the standard to which all human life is to be referred. If you did so, some most surprising results would follow. The sound socialist who constantly beats his children must be a better man than the old-fashioned capitalist (and there are some of them) who takes a genuine delight in helping other people. The good socialist instead of the good man must be your ideal. Personally I prefer the latter, even though I'm not sure what a good man is. Nor do I believe that you are sure.

'This brings us back to the point from which we started—your talk of free-will, and making a final choice, and settling now, in spite of all your inexperience, the course along which your life will proceed. I strongly distrust such exercises of free-will, and particularly so in your case; for you are entering on a plan which is bound to keep you in continual opposition to others. It may gratify your vanity for a time, but it will distort and dull your character.

'It is a monstrous thing to organize your life round one or two principles, particularly so if they are political principles. Suppose now you do as you say you will do and go in for politics, an extremist and proud of it. I could prophesy your future pretty accurately, but will leave that for the moment. First, let me hear your justification. Why is it that you propose to give up an ordinary career for which you're well equipped and become a proselytizing socialist? Why put socialism before all the

other things in life? You may say, because it strikes you
as being something "good." But where are your terms
of reference? You don't know what "good" means. You
may say that it is "satisfactory," that it "gives meaning"
to your life. So might a thousand other pursuits. There
are some people, I believe, who find their meaning in
the assumption that they are a superior race. Life is too
big to have meaning given to it so easily. The majority
of people can find plenty of meaning in their jobs and
in their personal relations. The few who are intelligent
enough to look for more meaning than this will look for
it in religion, art or philosophy.

'Honestly there seems to me to be something uncouth
and vulgar in your preoccupation with people's wages
and their standard of living. Certainly these things are
important, but they are trivial when compared with the
real depth and complexity of life. No doubt you get
into a great state when you think of the sufferings of the
unemployed: has it ever struck you how infinitesimal a
part of suffering in general is constituted by these particular sufferings? When man has done everything most
efficiently, most perfectly in accordance with his highest
principles, there will still remain death, the slow cor-
ruption of the beauty of body and mind, the million
vanities, affectations and deceits that are in the best of
us. Worse than this: there will always be the underlying
inscrutability and horror of things. Behind the most
enthusiastic shouting in the streets, the most admirable
and antiseptic programmes, behind elegant gestures and
conversation, behind the lover's kiss, is an awful noth-
ingness, and men will have lost all their wisdom if they
fail from time to time to perceive it.'

Here he stopped speaking suddenly and bit his lip, as though regretting the fervour of his last words. Charles was looking hard at him, as indeed was I. How rarely it was, I reflected, that people failed to speak the truth, and how strangely at variance, each from each, were the truths which they expressed!

Charles began to speak slowly, and there was less animation in his voice. 'You are like the devil,' he said, 'quoting scripture. Everything you say is right, or nearly so; but the result is all wrong, and to-day we must judge by results, however vulgar that may seem to you. There may have been times when you would have been right to be a spectator, never to move a step till everything had been mapped out in advance, and constantly able to consult your "terms of reference," as you call them. But now isn't one of those times. As for me, I know my terms of reference are incomplete, I know that life is bigger than politics, I know that people can be satisfied in different ways. But I can see hope in some directions, danger and despair and injustice in others. And one knows danger and injustice even if one is unable perfectly to define justice and security. Anyone can see the hopelessness and paralysis in which we live. We both saw it early in our lives, when we were at school during the last war. Ten million dead, you may say, is a small thing when viewed beside an infinity of space and time and experience. No doubt: but it is still too big for us to grasp. And, if any sign were wanting, that last war was sign enough that our civilization no longer deserved respect.'

Now he was speaking bitterly and he looked straight at me as he continued. 'Leave aside "the liberation of mankind," it's a good enough thing just to work to prevent another war like the last.'

'Prevent it, if you can,' said his friend, 'though personally I rather doubt your success. There are too many people about who like that form of excitement.' Then he sighed and rose to his feet. 'I must be going,' he said, 'and I see that you're determined to have your own way.

'Let me just indulge in a little prophecy. I can see you addressing meetings very ardently; but there'll be very much more ardour on the platform than anywhere else. "Comrades," you will say, and it will be no doubt very effective, but when you look round to see who your comrades are you will probably find them to consist of several old women with pacifist leanings, some schoolboys, a theorist or two, and perhaps a deaf old man who has been, as he will say, "in the movement" ever since he can remember. That is if you stay here. If you happen to work in a more "advanced" district, there will be more excitement, but it will mostly be occasioned by quarrels and intrigues amongst those who are supposed to be working with you.

'Meanwhile, perhaps, you will marry, as enthusiastic about this as about everything else. Almost certainly you will take this step when you have insufficient money to support a home. You will think it contemptible to demand standards of comfort which are much higher than the lowest. After a short time your devotion to "the cause" will lead you to neglect your wife, who, in all probability will have no use for "the cause" at all and will seek consolation elsewhere, and probably with some other man. You yourself, in self-defence, will grow

harder and more opiniated. You will despise people
like me, and that again will be a sign of weakness, for
we shall not despise you. We shall merely be sorry for
you. For whatever you may achieve will not be worth
the sacrifices which you will have made. There you are.
Tell me in fifteen years whether I was right or wrong.'

2

I looked quickly across the room at Charles to see how
he had been affected by his friend's forecast, but even
as I turned my eyes to him I saw that both his face and
posture were different.

Now his face frowned as he bent over a large piece of
paper upon which he was writing in short bursts of
energy, and from time to time would pause, bite the end
of his pen, smile sometimes or frown with deeper concentration and sometimes even turn and look up at me
who was standing behind the rickety wooden chair on
which he sat. It was a small and mean room in which
we were. There was a high window, through which I
could see the shutters half folded back with the grey
paint peeling from them and beyond the shutters the
rain falling across a blank wall; and by the window was
a tin washstand and a strip of carpet. An iron bedstead
was all the other furniture apart from the table and
chair at which the man was sitting. It might have been,
I thought, a room in some cheap and old-fashioned
hotel, perhaps abroad.

I looked over Charles' shoulder as he wrote and he
turned his head to me gravely, almost as though he
might be expecting me to be visible to him. His face
was older; indeed he looked now much the same as he
had done when I first saw him, except that his clothes

were ragged, his hair close-cropped, and that there was a wild look in his eyes which I had not seen there before. There was a yellow packet of cigarettes on the table in front of him and, as he wrote, he smoked one cigarette after another, from time to time knocking off the black ash on to the unswept floor. His handwriting, I noticed, was neat and meticulous, although he wrote fast. The beginning of the letter on which he was engaged was covered over by a loose sheet of paper, but before I had read many words I knew that they were addressed to that very friend to whom I had heard him speaking just now and yet so long ago.

'You will be glad to know,' I read, 'that I have been released. But I am not writing merely to tell you that. I am wondering whether perhaps you remember a conversation which we had fifteen years ago. On that occasion you made a prophecy about my future, and you asked me to tell you, after fifteen years, whether you had been right or wrong.

'In those days I used to think of you as the devil, since you were always right up to a point, and yet finally you were, to my manner of thinking, wholly wrong. I still think of you like that. Yet I see that the devil is even more accurate than I used to believe. The truths which you represent are real truths, more bitter and important than I was prepared to think them. Your prophecies are reliable; nearly all of them have been fulfilled.

'Yet what were they based upon? On acute analysis and the assumption that it is almost impossible to imagine crime, folly, stupidity and inhumanity of which human beings will not be capable, of which one will not be capable oneself. This you see clearly, and it is partly this which makes you feel that horror of life of which you once spoke with more emotion than you intended to express. But you would not feel the horror if you had not also felt or wished to feel the wonder and delight. You are like a person who looks at a beautiful face, with blood flushing the cheeks, honesty and adventure in the eyes, kind lips, everything which calls for love; but you will not see it so. You will take each feature separately, and envisage the appearance of the inside of the nose. You will be disgusted as you reflect upon what this face would be if the skin were removed from it. You will know that its bloom is nourished by processes of digestion and excretion which seem to you to fit very ill with the emotions that might be aroused at first glance and on insufficient evidence. You will be conscious of the fact that disease can mar the face, that years will certainly waste it, that finally, if left to itself, it will dissolve into shapelessness and putrefaction.

'And these reflections of yours will seem to you horrible and more than that. They will seem nearer to what you conceive of as "truth" than is the impression which this lovely face makes immediately upon the eye of a lover. At least you will say that the two views are equally true.

'How can I express myself? They are both true, but they are not equally so. There is more of what man was made for in the one than in the other. "An emotional attitude" you will say, and I reply that all attitudes are emotional, fed either by hope or by fear.'

Here he stopped writing and leaned back in his chair while he lit another cigarette. As he leaned back, he turned his head towards me and looked directly in my eyes gravely, as though questioning me as to the accuracy of what he had just written. As for me I was deeply moved by what I had seen him write, for the thoughts which he had been expressing reminded me of what I had seen at the moment of my death, that inviting prospect and the broken bodies on the shaking ground.

He turned suddenly away from me and again I looked over his shoulder and read as follows:

'I have often seen men die, both on our side and on the other, and I have often wondered what their feelings were when they became conscious that they were losing irrevocably every opportunity of life. Perhaps only a few of them ever presented the situation to themselves in this light, but of those who did and whose minds were at least partially undisturbed by pain I am convinced that most looked with an infinite regret on what they were leaving, and this even although they may never have enjoyed security or much obvious happiness while they were alive. Yet they had at some time, if only for a moment, imagined life as that beautiful face of which I was speaking, something which might fill a lover with reverence and desire.

'This may be true of all soldiers. I believe it was especially true of us who were fighting, most of us, for something in which we passionately believed. And this brings me to my final argument against you. It is true that in Spain and in the relations of other countries with Spain you will be able to find examples of every kind of meanness, cowardice, stupidity, savagery and malice. You may regard our defeat as evidence of the uselessness of our actions. But if you look farther you will see more. You will see, for example (if you will allow me in my turn to prophesy), that our defeat was the first action of a war in which, though you refused to intervene, you will very shortly be involved, when you will have to pay extravagantly for your pretence of impartiality.

'In the war which will shortly break out vast masses of men will be conscripted to fight, and they will be encouraged to fight by every artifice of propaganda. By every artifice, that is, except one which might have been of the utmost service. I am thinking of our story; and imagine that it will be unceremoniously and indecently forgotten, since the record with regard to us of those who will soon be crusading patriots will seem too shameful to bear publicity. It is a record which would seem to justify all the hatred and contempt which you used to express when we talked of "politics." "Leave all that" you used to say "to inferior minds and stunted characters. It's a dirty business." I tell you that in a few years you will see the result of your policy. When that time arrives, please remember what I am saying now.

'You will find then that every passion will be aroused against those very people who have just defeated us in Spain. What we said about them for years and what was disbelieved, blanketed or disregarded, will be trumpeted from the house tops. What will not be so widely publicized is this: that from every part of Europe there came to Spain as volunteers men who had realized the danger long ago and who, in most cases against the definite instructions of their governments, made the final bid to save the whole of Europe from what is now the inevitable war. These men were of all kinds. Some had grudges to pay off, some were over-dogmatic, some what you would call "enthusiasts," some were unfitted for fighting, being merely idealists. Some trusted in the sincerity of what we still call "the democratic powers." Yet I say without hesitation that among these men was the flower and the hope of Europe.

'However their record may be suppressed for purposes of policy, in the end they will be seen as the first army of the future, representatives of a hope and courage in man that cannot finally be dimmed. And this even now is what stands before my mind more clearly than the appalling sufferings, the devastation, the total defeat which we have experienced. A volunteer army was formed from men of all countries, all creeds, all types of upbringing and occupation. There were complicated theories, but finally there was one belief, in the possibility of a good and free life, one hatred—against injustice, tyranny, inhumanity and war.

'That is the lively centre of my picture and around it are grouped the horrors and the senilities of a dying world which have proved themselves still in this instance stronger than the infant future. In our country sat a committee of statesmen who from time to time assured us that the planes which blasted us from our positions did not exist. The process of beating us down by a superior weight of metal was described as neutrality. In the conduct of the Athenian envoys at Mitylene you will find a fine example of cynicism, but of cynicism so wrapped and folded in hypocrisy and irresolution I fancy that the finest example in history will be discovered in our own times.

'The broken fragments of our army escaped across the frontier into a country whose leaders had often expressed admiration for the ideals which had animated

us. There at this moment the majority of them are
rotting away in concentration camps. Their crime and
danger is that they have seen too clearly what is coming.
They must be put out of sight lest they cause offence.
And you may well be tempted to say "This is the final
and crowning act of cruelty and hypocrisy. This, if
nothing else, shows the futility of struggle, the worth-
lessness of the world." But I do not think so. The fact
that that army did exist still fills me with pride and
hope.

'The war that is coming will be a full-scale affair.
Great bodies of men and material will be set in motion
by representative assemblies. The same airmen who
bombed the sunny villages where we fought will unload
their bombs in much greater numbers on much larger
targets. Men will fight then for their own homes, and
splendid ideals will be set before them to encourage
them to fight the more resolutely. I am inclined, as I
said, to doubt whether what might most help them will
be put before them, the story of our army, who fought
from their own hearts on foreign soil, hoping for the
possibility of peace and believing in the dignity of man.
Yet our army existed and that is what matters.

'This, then, is my answer to your question of fifteen
years ago. You were wrong, though everything which
you said was true. There is more evil in men than I
believed: the horror of which you spoke is there. But
the hope and goodness which I envisaged then is real
too, and it is this for which man was made, and must
make himself.'

He sighed and laid down his pen on the table in front
of him. Then he rose from his chair and turned so that

he stood facing me. I could see that his face was deeply lined and that his eyes were grim. He looked hard at me, almost inquisitively, and then returned to his writing.

'There is a kind of razor-edge,' he wrote, 'between despair and hope, and that is where I seem to stand. I think of those who will fight and be killed in the next war. They will be caught up and involved in the vast machineries of modern states, and only a few of them, perhaps, will ever pause to consider why it is that they will lose their lives. Many will wonder what there is on either side that has shown itself deserving of such a sacrifice. Many will perform acts of extraordinary heroism and in their action will be animated only by the instincts of primitive tribesmen, or of simple men, loyal to each other, and accidentally finding themselves caught in a storm of steel. Yet their adventures will not be accidental. There must be understanding as well as courage, pity and fury for the past if these lives are not to be thrown away far more idly than were the lives of our army.

'I can imagine a situation of extraordinary complexity where the ordinary man will be bewildered by the difficulty of telling friend from foe. Yet if he fails to support his friends he will be entering again on the paths of cruelty and indifference which will lead to yet another war or else, what is as bad, to a perpetual subjection. I still believe in the goal—"the liberation of mankind," and this phrase is clearer to me now than it was in the days when it merely served to stir a generous emotional warmth. It is liberation both of the body and the mind. It is a recognition that the whole world—its material resources, its beauty, the intellectual achievements of its inhabitants—is the birthright of all men without distinction of race or creed or colour or ancestry or occupation. It is a belief that hatred and separation are normally the results of fear, and that love, confidence, respect and satisfaction are not unnatural. Certainly this is a creed that is mouthed by half the world. These were assumed to be the beliefs of those who threw my comrades into concentration camps. And such hypocrites may well prove more dangerous to us even than open and honest enemies who are disgusted by any such conception as mankind, and concentrate their energies on the self-importance of a particular nation, or class. But I have seen people die who were not hypocrites and who believed in these ideals.'

Again he laid down his pen and rose to his feet. As he did so, I found that the scene had changed and that once more I was standing at his side in the abbey, and that he was speaking with his eyes levelled at me.

'The enemies,' he was saying, 'do not believe in life on earth. What is the good of ideals that are as wide as the world, unless they are so passionately believed in that they result in action instead of dissipating themselves in day dreams?'

He glanced angrily at the priest who was standing with his head bowed, but who now looked up quickly in another direction, for the elderly woman in black had begun to speak, and there was a note of impatience in her voice.

'If your ideals were as wide as the world,' she said, 'they would not be so cruel. I know them. They take away from us the real happiness which we might have.'

As she spoke her eyes flashed and the blood rose to

her cheek. I saw that in her youth she must have been beautiful, and I began to wonder from what experience it was that she spoke so bitterly of the firmly held beliefs which I had just heard expressed. Certainly Charles had not answered my question, but he had impressed me greatly as being the only one of the sightseers who seemed to have given any thought at all to the predicament in which I found myself. He was unique among the rest also in having spent a great part of his life in attempting consciously to prevent the catastrophe in which I and so many others had been overwhelmed; and, if he had been unsuccessful, it did not necessarily follow that he had been wrong. I could sympathize with him in his struggle for a world that would be just and peaceful, and, like him, regarded as heroes those who had laid down their lives, against hopeless odds, with this end in view. I could sympathize also with the views which his friend, 'the devil,' had expressed: for I had seen simultaneously the width and wonder of a world together with its crippling and disruption.

Yet I could not fail to remember that in warfare it is seldom that one side has a monopoly of the belief in the justice of its cause. For my own part I remembered that our thoughts were more concerned with the defeat of the enemy than with any precise ideas as to the organization of society after the war. Indeed, when we thought of peace, our minds were occupied with simpler and perhaps more selfish desires than the planning of a better world. Nor could I believe that our imaginations were wholly misdirected; for, admirable as is the vision of ordered justice, it seemed to me to lack something of the colour, intricacy and delight of what I had seen when I died. Even justice, I thought, might be a small element in the totality of existence, and those whose thoughts were too strictly concentrated upon it might dismiss as 'daydreams' other elements in the whole which were at least as important.

Was it, I wondered, some such a feeling as this that lay behind the words of the woman in black. And, as I looked at her, I saw that her face and manner were no longer what they had been when I saw them first.

CHAPTER VII

The Woman

1

I WAS looking now at the face of a young woman, and, for myself, I found that my feet were on the black surface of a towing path which followed the winding course of a river along which there were three of us walking in the rays of a setting sun.

The girl at my side stopped suddenly and, turning away from me, gripped her companion's arm. 'Oh, look!' she said. 'Look!' And in her voice both excitement and a kind of reverence were curiously blended.

I followed the direction of her outstretched hand and saw skimming the shining surface of the water, past the sedges and the cavernous opening of a boathouse and the earthy river banks now reddened by the sun's departing glow, like a jewelled dart flying, the flashing shape of a kingfisher following the river in a breathless instant till he rounded the bend. We stood still for a moment after the bird had disappeared, and then the girl looked up into her companion's face and he looked at her, still silent. It appeared to me that they were in love, amazed with the excitement of it, and that they

146

regarded this phenomenon of nature, this flying bird,
as some kind of a mystery or sacrament whose appearance filled them with wonder and delight, binding them
even more closely together than heretofore.

I studied the girl's face, her wide confident eyes and
honest brow, her half-opened lips and the tender flesh
of her throat rising from the neck of the light green
summer dress which she was wearing. As I watched her
she threw back her head and laughed, shaking as she
did so, the fair curls of hair which hung down at the
sides of her cheeks, beneath the broad rim of her hat
I hardly noticed the strangeness, to my eyes, of this
article of clothing, for what most impressed me was the
spirit and delicacy of the girl. I had never seen, in the
whole course of my enquiry, such evident happiness.
There was nothing of afterthought, reservation or eva-
sion in the young woman's eyes. I looked long at her,
and was happy myself in her existence.

In the face of the man at her side there was a more
sober, but at least equal, joy. He too was young and
it was the youth and freshness of him which took my
notice rather than his high-cut jacket and the straw hat
which he carried in one hand. His eyes were fixed on
the woman's, and his lips were smiling. He looked
round him quickly, over the empty meadows and the
path behind us; then kissed the girl on the mouth. I
saw the muscles of her neck stir as she leaned her face
towards him, and then heard her laugh as their bodies
drew apart and they continued their walk, silently, with
me keeping pace with them in the soft evening air.

In front of us was a lock gate, a dark wall, since the
sun was behind the gate; little spurts and runnels of

water broke here and there the tall black surface; and to the right of the lock was a small island, with willows bowed over the water. The air was so still that clouds of gnats could be seen easily, rising and falling by the island banks, while above and below them swooped and circled the quick shapes of swallows and martins. One could hear, and just glimpse, beyond the island the rush of water from a weir. There the stream whitened and curled and hurried away, but hardly disturbed the even current on our side of the drooping willows.

The red brick of the lock-keeper's cottage glowed and flushed in the late light, and the flowers in his garden too, salvia, snapdragon and massive begonia, like separate sources of illumination, bathed and drenched the ground with their bright and different colours by the black water and the cool green of the trees. To the right of us were the open golden meadows with here and there cattle feeding in them, and to our left was rising ground, fenced off by railings, grassy slopes where stiff-standing oak trees grew and white deer grazed or delicately rubbed their sides against the wrinkled bark of the trees.

By the railings was a wooden seat, and here the man and the woman sat down, while I stood close to them, looking now at them and now at the tranquil summer scene. I saw that the man lightly rested his hand on the woman's knee. 'Are you happy?' he asked, and I smiled, for to one who could see the exaltation both in her face and in his the question must have seemed unnecessary. Yet, as I knew, such questions will always be asked of each other by lovers who seek every confirmation which word or gesture can supply of their deeply-felt bewildered delight, who would share together each momentary spark of pleasure, each sudden recognition of their peace, and who, in some part of them, perhaps, ardently desire to hold and fix by word or action the amazing present lest it should vanish into what they know of the past or suspect of the future.

The girl leaned forward and rubbed her eyes with her hands. She smiled, and then, with her gaze fixed upon the gentle flow of the river, her face became graver as she spoke slowly. 'I've never been so happy,' she said. 'I never believed that one could be so happy. It makes one tremble.'

The man looked down at her tenderly. 'I know what you mean,' he said. 'There seem to be all kinds of opposites inside one. But they aren't fighting among themselves, as you might expect. It's like the lion and the lamb lying down side by side. There's agitation and peace together, a kind of wildness and a tenderness that might be for handling spider's webs. There's something, as you say, that makes one tremble, but there's a deeper confidence, so that one doesn't tremble at all. I don't anyway.'

He laughed and she sat up, looked into his eyes and leaned her face towards him. Then she turned her head away and remained gazing at the river.

The sun had now set, though the flowers still glowed with what seemed to be their own light. In the distance I could hear a dog barking and this sound made me the more conscious of the deep silence into which it had broken. I looked closely at the young man who was leaning back in the seat and who now looked up at me with a curiously hesitant expression in his eyes. He continued to look at me as he said in a voice which might have been either serious or joking:

'Have we the right to be so happy?'

The girl sat up quickly and took his face between her two hands. I noticed that a quick expression of fear or worry had passed over her face, like a rapid cloud over a piece of sunny ground. Then she smiled. 'Of course,' she said. 'What good would we be to ourselves or anyone else if we were miserable?' She looked eagerly at him and smiled as she saw the expression of his face change. 'What were you thinking of?' she asked, as she dropped her hands, and, with a quick impulsive gesture, shook her head in half-mocking disapproval. There was, in spite of a superficial merriment, anxiety and more than a girl's tenderness in her eyes.

The man took one of her hands in his. 'Nothing,' he said. 'I know it's good for us to be happy like this. More good than anything in the world.'

I noticed that, though the words were spoken confidently, there was something of desperation in the tones of his voice and still an uneasiness in his bearing of which the woman was no doubt even more aware than I was.

'It is something,' she said, 'and you ought to tell me. I know what it is.'

For a moment or two she looked away from him over the river and meadows which seemed now darker and emptier than before. The air was colder and now a small breeze just ruffled the surface of the stream. The man rose to his feet.

'Yes,' he said, 'you're right.' He looked at her tenderly and again smiled, but she, as she too rose, did not smile

in answer to him. Her face was anxious and perplexed
and frightened, although I saw that she was making an
effort to control her feelings.

'It's the war you're thinking of,' she said, as we began
to walk away from the lock gates, and the brilliant
flowers.

Her companion nodded his head as she took his arm.
I took my place at his side as we moved slowly along the
path to a bridge in the distance and the houses of a
village street.

Before long the man spoke again, nervously, but yet
with a kind of assurance which showed that he had
already thought much of what he was saying. 'My
dearest,' he said, 'there is nothing in the world which
I love like I love you. And there is no happiness on
earth that can compare with what I feel when I am
with you.'

He paused, but the woman at his side made no sign
of having heard his words. She was looking fixedly at
the ground, a frown of concentration on her face.

The man continued to speak and said, as he glanced
sidelong at me: 'You know this, and yet I can't help
thinking of the fellows over there.'

He was going on further in his speech, but the girl
interrupted him. 'I know,' she said. 'Of course one can't
help thinking of them. It's terrible and pitiable, but it's
wicked too.' She clutched his arm and began to speak
with greater urgency, and I noticed that, as she spoke,
the man's face became harder and from time to time he
turned away from her imploring eyes, looking either
towards me or the darkening river.

'How many of them,' she asked, 'want to kill each

other? How many of them are young boys with the whole of life opening out to them, and they are having it taken from them by the old men who have forgotten how to be happy? How many of them are men like you who love their wives and who have wives who love them? Oh, I know that they are heroes, but they are so stupid. What sensible person wants to conquer countries nowadays? What do we want except peace and quiet and love?'

The young man spoke again, very gently but somehow a little pompously, although I saw that there was much sincerity of feeling behind his words. 'Exactly, dearest,' he said. 'We are all agreed on that. But it may be necessary to fight for these things. Not only for ourselves, but for our children.'

Here he gripped her more tightly by the arm and spoke with an added tenderness, while she seemed to shudder as she shook her head in disagreement. He did not observe her gesture and went on speaking as though she were at a greater distance than in fact was the case.

'It's this militarism,' he said. 'We've got to put an end to it. And I can't help thinking that it's selfish of us to let other fellows take all the risks while we enjoy ourselves at home. We ought to help too, if we approve of what they're doing.'

The girl looked up quickly and I saw that tears were in her eyes. 'I don't approve,' she said. 'Oh, I don't, I don't approve.' Her voice was like a cry, but as she turned her head to the man she could see that her words had had little or no effect on him. His face was grim and unhappy as he strode by my side with his eyes fixed on the slow stream.

The woman took his arm and hugged it till the severity of his expression relaxed. 'My dearest,' she said. 'Let's wait till we get home. Let's not talk about it now.'

He smiled indulgently at her and we continued to walk on toward the bridge in silence; but now, as we moved slowly forward, there was little in our mood of that ecstasy in which even I had shared just now, when we were walking in the opposite direction. No doubt the love between the lovers was as deep as before, but they were aware now of something else, something blank and impenetrable, like an iron wall, which shut off the man from the woman. They would never again with precisely the same unreflecting confidence stand together as they had stood and watched the kingfisher. However they might in the future bless the chance which had brought them together, they would still be conscious of their ultimate separation.

So I thought as we approached the houses of the village, still silent, and stepped off the towing path into a street that wound steeply up a hill.

But before the hill there was a level expanse of grass, a village green, with great elm trees around it, except for that portion which was closest to the river, where a public house stood. It was an old building, with an archway opening into a yard, and I observed that in the wooden beams of the archway house-martins had made their nest. Even in this late light a mother-bird hung on furiously flapping wings in front of the tiny aperture in her mud building through which craned the necks of her young. The small birds cried into the chilling air and from time to time one or other of the men who were seated below at narrow deal tables with glass tankards in their hands would point out to his companions the agitation of the birds and make some comment upon it in a voice which I could not hear.

The deal tables were almost on the grass and within ear-shot of a performance which was taking place in the centre of the small village green. Here a farm cart had been set to make a platform. Around it stood villagers with brass instruments of music, and on it was an elderly man in a frock coat who was making a speech to the small audience which was gathered near him. I could hear plainly that he was appealing to them to enlist in the armed forces, and I observed on the platform from which he was speaking posters of a kind which I had seen revived in my own lifetime.

There could be no doubt of the fervour of the orator as he spoke confidently beneath the elm trees in the light of the setting sun; yet to me there was something quaint in the procedure, something which only partly answered to my memory of the days of mobilization which I personally had known. For on this past occasion it appeared that people could remain, if they wished, outside the war, and I began to wonder for how long this system could continue.

The man and woman whom I accompanied were passing by the tables where the men sat drinking. Some of these raised their hands in greeting as we went by, and the woman acknowledged their greeting by a smile. But the man at her side had his face turned from them. He was staring at the cart in the centre of the patch of grass and listening intently to the words, ordinary enough as they were, which the speaker uttered. I could distinguish clearly enough phrases with which I too had been familiar: 'Our boys out there,' 'a final and glorious peace,' 'the justice of our cause,' 'the malice of our enemies.'

The young man paused and it was evident that he would have liked to listen, at least for a moment or two. He turned to the woman at his side and saw, as I did, in her face so much of anxiety and despair that he could not bear to detain her from the place where she wanted to be. His face set somewhat harder and we turned away to the left, past the speaker and the brass band, and began to ascend the hill.

We went slowly, and without speaking a word, past red brick cottages and stopped in front of one which was distinguished from the rest by having a cherry tree planted in its small front garden. Here the man relinquished the woman's arm and advanced to unlock the door. I followed the two of them into a parlour rather larger and better furnished than one would have expected to find in so small a dwelling. There were comfortable arm-chairs, an oak table and dresser, bookcases against the wall and, on the window sill, a vase of flowers. The window itself was a small one with leaded panes, so that the light inside the room was dim and I could hardly see the faces of the two whom I was accompanying until the man had lit a candle on the table and two others on the chimney piece. Then the soft golden light glowed from polished surfaces and shone on the faces which I wished to see.

The man turned round from the fireplace and I saw that the expression in his eyes was both softer and sadder than it had been when we were on our way up the hill. He stretched out his arms towards the woman and she hastened towards him, and so they stood for some moments clasping each other in a gesture which was no doubt symbolic of the identity of interest and purpose which they hoped and even expected to find together as a bond additional to their mutual affection. It was a welcome, but somewhat sad embrace, and, when they had drawn apart, I could see that there were tears in the woman's eyes.

For a second she let her hand rest on the man's sleeve, then removed the hat from her head and sat down in one of the chairs in front of the fireplace. She leaned forward and extended her hands to the flames flickering among the logs there; her face, I thought, in the light from the fire and candles, was older than it had seemed when we were walking by the river. But the severity of her expression was softened by the mild light, so that there was a tenderness and charity about her which I found infinitely endearing.

'Let me say what I mean now,' she said, and there was a strange resolution and confidence in her slow voice.

The man sat down in the chair opposite to her, leaning back in it and surveying her face which seemed unconscious of his scrutiny.

'My dear,' she said, 'I think I know what you are thinking. Perhaps I don't quite understand it, and I'm sure you don't quite understand what *I* think. It's the horror of it all, all that slaughter and cruelty and crime and separation and disease—all that is so great that I can't see how it can possibly be justified. I know that we say that we're right and they're wrong; but the difference between us can't be so stupendous as to make all this right.'

Here she made a gesture with her hand in my direction. She was speaking earnestly and yet somewhat desperately, as though, do what she might, she was unable perfectly to express herself.

The man broke in and spoke kindly, as if humouring her. 'Of course I see all that, dear,' he said. 'Of course it wouldn't be justified unless this were a war to end war.'

He too looked quickly at me, and then turned his eyes gravely on the woman. It seemed that he imagined that he had said something final.

'I don't believe it,' she said. 'Look at the way this was started. Anyone might have set it going, anywhere, at any moment. It was a kind of general condition of disease all over Europe, and no one did anything to cure it. And we're not curing it now. It is just taking its course. I believe that the millions who are suffering from it are mostly people like you and me, who hate the whole idea of it and who just want to live and find happiness with each other.'

Again she paused and looked across the fireplace at her companion. There was a slow and sad smile on her face. He too smiled, but rather bitterly.

'I am afraid,' he said, 'that you take much too charitable a view of the enemy. After all, there's plenty of evidence that they've been behaving like wild beasts.'

While he was speaking these words there was a look of ferocity on his face which I had not seen before. I noticed that the woman surveyed him almost with dismay before she broke in indignantly.

'Atrocities! Yes, that's part of the disease. Men *will* behave like wild beasts when they are maddened by fear and unreality. On both sides it will be the same thing. Haven't you got to behave like a wild beast when you charge with a bayonet?'

He did not answer this question. Instead he spoke with a note of anger in his voice. 'You're all mixed up,' he said. 'You're arguing as though I was maintaining that war is a good thing. Of course it isn't. I agree with you absolutely about all the horrors of it. But that isn't the point. The point is that it's actually going on, and it seems to me selfish to stand outside and make laments instead of doing something about it.'

Either the tone of his voice, or the words themselves, or both had hurt her. She stood as though mystified, and repeated to herself some of the phrases which he had used—'doing something' and 'it seems selfish.' Then she turned to him and spoke more passionately than before. I could see her eyes dilate and the muscles about her mouth harden.

'Do you think it's selfish,' she said, 'the way I feel about you? Oh, surely you must understand. It's good and not selfish at all. There's nothing in my heart but love, and not only love for you and the baby we are having, but for everything and everyone. I felt this love just then, when we were standing by the river and saw the kingfisher. I felt the goodness and beauty that there is in everything and that one can see, when one's heart is full of love. So you must have felt; and then suddenly you have forgotten it all. But I am faithful to that feeling of love and joy. And how can I think of war and wounds and savagery and pride and dullness when

I feel as I do? I know that there is something vast and wicked and cruel and mechanical which has somehow entrapped millions and which is trying to entrap you. It is cold and proud and dull in spite of all the splendid ideals with which it clothes itself. I hate these ideals which are only mentioned when it is a question of persuading men to kill each other. I have only to look into my heart to see something finer than all of them. You may talk of "duty to one's country," "loyalty," "sacrifice," even "duty to one's fellowmen"; but to me these are meaningless and hypocritical words when I see the kind of actions to which they lead and when I compare them with the duty which I feel and love, the duty to what is best in my heart and to the joy and love and beauty in all the universe.'

She looked hard at him, pleadingly; and, as she looked, saw at once how helpless she was. For his face expressed a kind of paternal sympathy for her beliefs, but no acknowledgment of them. So they remained for a moment or two in silence and it occurred to me that this young woman, who, to judge from her clothes, was implicated in a war earlier than the one in which I had lost my life, was thinking in a way not at all unlike the way in which I had thought at the moment of my death. I too had seen a vision of surprising and entrancing beauty whilst at the same moment I saw my body abject and broken among the broken bodies of my fellows.

The incongruity of the two views was what still perplexed me, and this same incongruity, presented only in the imagination, was evidently so shocking to the woman in front of me that she was unable to imagine it as part of the nature of things. Her life had seemed full, fascinating and extensive; yet now she was plunged into an element that was incomprehensible to her. I sympathized deeply with her in her confident faith which would still not bring her happiness.

The man was looking sadly at her. 'I feel what you say,' he said, 'but I feel other things too. Would you have me different from what I am?'

For a moment she looked at him with the utmost compassion. Then her eyes filled with tears. She covered her face with her hands and went quickly out of the room.

The man took a pace forward as though to follow her. But it seemed that he realized that further argument would be unfruitful and even comfort, at the moment, misplaced. He stepped back again to the fireplace and sat down. For some seconds he stared into the fire, and then took up as it were idly with one hand a copy of an illustrated magazine from a table at his side. As he turned over the leaves I noticed what seemed to me quaint photographs of bearded generals, of horses galloping madly as in long teams they drew small and old-fashioned guns, of antiquated warships and of royal personages. The man looked intently at these photographs, and when, in his perusal of the magazine, he came upon a recruiting advertisement, he surveyed it thoughtfully for some time.

Then he turned his head so that he looked directly into my eyes. As he looked at me so intently I found that his face, in spite of its intentness, was fading from my sight, and the scene changing.

2

I was in the same room, but now it was bright daylight and neither the man nor the woman whom I had seen there was still present. I was standing by the window and, in front of me, near the empty fireplace were two elderly ladies speaking together in subdued tones. They were both standing, and from time to time would glance upwards at the ceiling of the room as though they were expecting something or other to emerge from it. I could just hear what seemed to me to be the crying of a baby from an upper room of the house. One of the two ladies addressed the other in a voice which was audible to me.

'One can't help feeling, Florence,' she said, 'that this kind of thing is extraordinarily sad. So young. We must do our best to show our sympathy.' She added, as though by way of an afterthought, 'And I am very sorry.'

The speaker was a small woman who wore a very tight costume of grey tweed. Round one of her arms was a band of black and on the top of her head was perched a small hat from which protruded a long pheasant's feather. Her face was small and resolute. The tight lips and rather large aquiline nose, together with her curious headgear, made her appear like the caricature of some military figure. She spoke in short determined sentences and, at the close of her speech, she would press her lips together with an air of finality. Only an occasional nervous flicker of a muscle at the corner of the mouth, and a slight tremulousness in her thin hands suggested a frailty that her whole manner tended to control and to suppress.

The woman whom she had addressed as 'Florence'

differed from her in almost every respect. She was big-boned and plump. The costume she wore was in bright and even garish colours of red and green. Her remark-ably red cheeks gave her an appearance of health which was suggested also by the large strong gestures she would make with her arms and indeed by her whole bearing. Her eyes were honest and direct. She spoke in a ringing voice.

'Of course, Caroline,' she said, 'it's sad. Personally I hate these visits of sympathy. It would be much better, I always think, if we could just get down on our haunches and howl, as I believe they do in certain primitive tribes. Much more sincere, if you see what I mean. And it would develop a fine community spirit among the women.'

The other lady, Caroline, had looked particularly grim at the mention of the word 'haunches.' Now she spoke sharply.

'Don't be so ridiculous, Florence. One of the advan-tages of civilization and education is that we can use words which mean something. We can encourage those who are bereaved to feel patriotically. We can point out the reasons why they must feel pride as well as sorrow.'

The large woman threw back her head and made a sound that was between that of a yawn and a sigh. 'All very well later on,' she said, 'but not at the beginning. At the beginning give me a good howl.' Then she spoke in a slightly lower voice. 'We don't want to pile on the patriotism here. Mrs. Barnes has only been married for a short time and she thinks much more of loving her husband than of winning the war.'

The woman whom I knew as Caroline stiffened her

neck and sniffed as though she had detected some suspicious smell. 'We must tell her,' she said, 'that her husband would not wish her to feel like this.'

As she spoke the door of the room opened slowly. I was standing opposite the door and it was on myself first of all that the eyes of the young married woman, who now entered, were directed. There was so profound a change in her appearance from what it had been when I had seen her last that I wished with all my heart I were visible to her so that I might approach her and attempt to console her for her loss. Yet, even had this been possible, what consolation could I have offered?

It was conceivable, I thought, that one of the few convictions which might now give her comfort was the unlikeliness of another war in which the young baby whom she held in her arms might be involved. Yet I, if I were able at all to explain my presence, could only do so at the cost of dissipating this illusion. So I was glad that, though she looked hard at me, she could see nothing. But I felt sorrow too, not only for her, but for my own wife and mother whose future feelings I began dimly to understand from this example of the past. Indeed in thirty years what depth and volume of women's sorrow must have encompassed the whole globe like a rolling sea of grief! Yet it had proved no impediment to fiercer feelings either in their sex or in ours. It seemed that we had miraculously marched to war over these waves of agony and had been for the most part unconscious of their depth.

The young woman in front of me was wearing black, and this colour served to emphasize the extreme pallor of her face, in which the eyes stood out unnaturally large and bright. There were lines about her mouth which I had not observed before and, seeing them now, I could well imagine how she must have stood, perhaps yesterday, at the street door of her cottage and received from some postal official the news of her husband's death. I could see her in my mind's eye, how she would have staggered back into the room, careless of appearances, and have clenched one hand convulsively and thrust it against her teeth. She would have been stupefied with grief and still was so, though now she made some effort to control herself, partly for the sake of her visitors, but more, probably, for the sake of the baby whom she carried in her arms, and who looked up into her face with a sleepy expression and a small smile of pure contentment.

After she had looked at me she turned her head down to the child whom she was carrying, and for a moment her face took on an expression of tranquillity. Then she looked up quickly at her two visitors, and stood still, as though nervous of approaching nearer and frightened of their presence. There was no welcoming smile on her face. Indeed she seemed rather trapped in some place where she had no business to be than the mistress of the house in which she stood.

The elder of the two ladies who had been called 'Caroline' spoke abruptly and in commanding tones.

'We have taken the liberty of calling,' she said, 'to offer our sympathy.' But there was no response whatever in the pale face of the woman to whom this sympathy was being offered. The lady smiled rather grimly and added, 'And to try and buck you up.'

The other lady, Florence, looked disapprovingly at

her companion. She stepped forward to the young mother and laid her hand on her arm, keeping it there although the other seemed to shrink away from her touch.

'What a beautiful baby!' she said. 'May I hold him?' And, as she spoke, the baby reached out his arms and pulled her nose, looking gravely at her.

The mother clung to her child as though both she and it had been threatened by the proposal just made. Then she grudgingly relinquished it, looking hard all the time at the big woman in the red and green costume who began to make deep chuckling noises in her throat.

'Tell me,' said Caroline briskly, 'did you have a telegram from the War Office?'

Mrs. Barnes looked at her intently and opened her mouth as though to reply. But from the expression of her eyes it seemed as though she had not heard the question. Finally she said 'Do sit down,' and, after a long pause pronounced the words, 'It is very kind.'

Caroline sat down firmly in one of the chairs by the fireplace and her friend, with the baby, in another. Mrs. Barnes came to the window where I was standing. She walked slowly, as though in her sleep, and sat down on the low seat at my side. She watched the baby closely, but from time to time would turn her eyes up to my face and, as I looked at them, they seemed, for all their brightness, hollow and unseeing.

The large lady who held the baby was the next to speak. 'It's no use just saying one's sorry, my dear,' she said. 'You know that, and none of us can be as sorry as you are. But if we can be of any practical help, I do hope you'll let us know. Taking the baby out, for instance.

I'd like that. Or gardening. I love it. And I say, would you like some apples? I've got tons and tons.' She spoke enthusiastically and, as she spoke, dug the baby in the ribs with her forefinger, while he laughed delightedly. 'Healthy little fellow,' said Florence. 'You get much more fun out of a baby than you do out of a dog, though dogs are less trouble.'

The young woman at my side kept her eyes on her child. She seemed still hardly to hear the words which were addressed to her and it was somehow surprising when she opened her lips and said: 'Thank you.'

The other lady now spoke abruptly. 'Come, come, my dear,' she said. 'You must really try to buck yourself up. I know it's difficult. But it must be done. For your own sake. For your baby's sake. For the sake of the whole country. It's a hard duty which we women have, to keep bucked up in spite of everything. But we owe it to the men who are fighting for us.'

She looked enquiringly at the young woman's face and was evidently taken aback by the depth of misery and perplexity which she saw there, feelings upon which her words had had no effect whatever. She leaned forward in her chair and whispered to Florence, but loudly enough for me to hear her, 'A terribly sad case.'

Florence, who was still dandling the baby, turned her head sharply and smiled at the uncomprehending face at my side. 'You know she's right, my dear,' she said, 'though I know it sounds cruel and unfeeling; and of course things don't happen all at once. I mean Rome wasn't built in a day. You must try and keep yourself fit. There's no doubt about it. Think of all the other women who are suffering too.' She paused and then quickly, as though she had suddenly remembered an important point which should have been mentioned earlier, added the words, 'Of course that ought to make things worse, oughtn't it? But really I think it makes them better. Very funny.'

There was an evident kindliness in the woman's face, and I saw that Mrs. Barnes was attempting to smile in a kind of acknowledgment of it; but no sooner did the muscles of her mouth move than her eyes filled with tears, and for a moment she leaned her head on her hands, wiping with her fingers the corners of her eyes.

The lady with the pheasant's feather in her hat spoke emphatically. 'Of one thing,' she said, 'you may be sure. Your man's death will be avenged. Personally I'm not at all sorry for those people. I think they deserve everything that we can do against them. When I think of all the suffering which they have caused I can't help hardening my heart. It may not be Christian, but I can't help it. And I believe there is such a thing as "righteous indignation." Never mind. I'd just like to have them all here. I'd make them sorry.'

She glared fiercely round the room, almost as though estimating its capacity to receive the large numbers of her enemies.

The young woman at my side spoke clearly for the first time, though her voice was very low. 'How can you be so evil?' she said. 'How can you be so evil?' She remained staring at the ground, as though she had been speaking to herself, but there was such conviction in her words that her two visitors were momentarily startled.

Florence was the first to speak. 'Oh, I say,' she exclaimed, 'isn't that rather a strong word? Of course what one really wants is an end to it all. But, after all, they started it. They'll have to be punished. Otherwise they'll do it again, don't you see?'

Mrs. Barnes looked up at her and began to speak slowly, with a puzzled expression on her face. 'I don't understand,' she said. 'I only know that I was happy and that I had a baby coming. And all over the world there were people like me. We hadn't done anyone any harm. We were happy. And now everywhere people are killing and maiming each other. I don't think it's heroic. I don't care whose fault it is. I know that it's evil.'

Both the women were looking kindly at her, but they seemed embarrassed for an answer. Finally the elder of the two, Caroline, said:

'I am a general's daughter, and I can assure you that my father disliked war. But there is such a thing as duty We must never forget that.'

The young woman let her expressionless eyes rest for a moment on the speaker's face. 'There is such a thing as love,' she said, and, as she spoke, again the tears welled up into her eyes. Her face fell forward on her hands as she began to sob desperately and unashamedly.

Florence, with the baby, rose quickly to her feet and began to pat the young woman on the back. 'There, there,' she said. 'Have a good cry. It will do you good.'

The other lady had also risen from her chair. She stood by the fireplace, surveying the woman's grief, and her lips were more than ever compressed, as though she were determined to avoid in herself any corresponding weakness. 'Poor thing!' she said. 'Poor thing!' and spoke rather as if she were giving an order. 'It will get better.'

She began vigorously to rub her upper lip, under the nose, with a forefinger held horizontally.

Mrs. Barnes began to speak through her tears, disjointedly, and sobbing between her sentences. But she still spoke slowly so that there was nothing hysterical about her utterance.

'Please leave me,' she said. 'I know you mean to be kind. You are kind. But it is no good. You don't see things as I see them. No one does.' And she raised her eyes to my face as though calling me to witness her words.

For my part I imagined that she might be thinking of that one moment when I had seen her and her dead husband standing by the river in the diffused light of evening, when they had watched in wonder the kingfisher flash across the glorious and tranquil scene. I too had seen such a vision, and perhaps even more clearly than had this woman, since I had beheld it in immediate and severe contrast with the fact of my real dissolution. This was still my perplexity, as it was hers; for how could she have imagined that the enchanting path which she had seen extend before her feet was in fact impassible for her, ground that was for ever forbidden? Both she and I, perhaps would have been happier if we had never known the possibility of happiness and envisaged the reality of beauty and of peace. And yet we would not exchange our uneasy knowledge for the more assured ignorance of others.

I pitied this young wife from the bottom of my heart; and I pitied also her elderly women visitors, who were perplexed by the sight of a sorrow which they could not wholly understand and, however clumsily, tried sincerely to alleviate it by using words which neither to the young woman nor to me had any very definite meaning.

The lady in the red and green costume had restored the baby to its mother. 'We'll leave you now,' she said. 'We didn't want to upset you. Don't forget about the apples.' And she squeezed Mrs. Barnes' hand affectionately as she went towards the door.

The other lady tapped the ground with her walking-stick. 'Courage!' she said somewhat indistinctly, and seemed to be addressing rather the walls of the room than anyone in particular. She closed softly the front door as she went out and I saw from the window both her and her friend walk in silence down the short garden path, past the cherry tree and into the street.

Mrs. Barnes had risen to her feet as her visitors left. She stood still, holding the baby tightly clutched against her breast and with the tears still running down her cheeks. I saw the baby wonderingly, as young children will, extend one hand towards her face and begin with his small finger to trace the course of a tear. His mother had been staring wildly at the window, but she was immediately conscious of the child's touch and turned down her eyes to meet his puzzled look.

'Oh my treasure,' she said, 'my little love. You will grow up into a better world.' And she looked suddenly at me as though something had startled her. 'Oh God!' she said, 'let me keep him! Let me love him! Let him be happy!'

Still she kept her eyes on me, and her eyes were fierce with sorrow. I turned my head aside so as not to see her, for, if I had been able to speak, I could have said nothing which would bring her any comfort.

There had been a time once, though now it seemed
to me very long ago, when I had been temporarily attached to some troops who were guarding an advanced
landing field. The enemy put in a counter attack which
for about twenty-four hours gave us a very awkward
time; though, in the end, we managed to hold them up
until we were strongly reinforced by our own tanks.
After it was all over we had some kind of a celebration.

I remember that Captain Wallace, who at this time
was still alive, had made friends with a fighter pilot of
whom we saw a lot, since he had been wounded and for
some days had been unable to fly. At the celebration
which we had after our repulse of the enemy I remember hearing this airman talk to Captain Wallace about
his mother. She had been against his joining the Air
Force, he said, since she had been by way of being a
pacifist. Captain Wallace had replied politely that at
one time he had been a pacifist himself.

The fighter pilot had looked at him gravely and said,
if I remember correctly: 'It's a mess all right, and often
now I wish I had time to think. But I suppose one
would call it a man's life. It's a sort of do or die existence, and that somehow seems better than the slow
decay that was going on before the show started. I suppose I thought that anything was better than that, and
perhaps I was right. But my mother was right too in a
way. Maybe some time one will be able to think things
out.'

Wallace had seemed to approve of this statement and
had said something to the effect that after the war he
intended to support some scheme of federalism; but, in

point of fact, neither he nor I nor the young airman ever saw the end of the war.

A few days later we heard that he had been shot down in combat and killed. He had had a fairly distinguished career and was posthumously awarded some decoration or other.

I mention this incident from my real life because now what I saw before my eyes and what surprised me was a photograph of this very fighter pilot whom I knew to be dead.

I was in a room which I had not seen before, a bedroom in which the curtains had been drawn across the windows and the electric light was still on. I was standing at the foot of the bed and what had immediately arrested my eyes was the photographs on a bed table. There was a photograph of the young woman and her baby whom I had just seen and, beside this, was a photograph of the fighter pilot. As I looked closely at it I could see resemblances between the face and the faces both of the young woman, Mrs. Barnes, and of her husband with whom I had seen her stand by the river. It also occurred to me, what I had forgotten, that this had, in fact, been the young man's name.

I looked now at the bed itself and saw sleeping there, though uneasily, the boy's mother. She was much older than when I had seen her last and indeed appeared almost of the same age as she actually was now, standing with me among the sightseers in the cathedral, although in the relaxation of sleep her face seemed less severe and less controlled than it was when she was awake.

From time to time she would shift the position of her body in bed or would quickly turn her head from side

to side. Her lips also moved continually as though she
was speaking, and I guessed that she had fallen to sleep
out of sheer exhaustion, since she had not even turned
out the light, and that now her sleep was far from being
as restful as it should be.

I looked with interest and affection at the sleeping
face and remarked how much it had changed from the
time when I had seen it bright with joy and wonder, by
the river in the summer light. And as I looked I heard
the words which came fluently from her moving lips,
though whether these words were in the strict sense
audible, or whether what she was saying to herself was
in some inexplicable manner engraved also on the
register of my own mind, it would be difficult to state
certainly. But the effect was as though I were listening
to a monologue, and this is what she was saying. I
watched her closely as she spoke, though from time to
time I would glance too at the photograph of her son,
since it moved me strangely so to be reminded of him.

'How strange it is,' she was saying, 'that when I am
asleep I can make long speeches in which I seem to be
able to say clearly what I mean to say, whereas in real
life I am often at a loss for words. Perhaps it is because
there is no one listening, or perhaps really I am not
talking sense at all, but only think I am doing so. Sometimes I make up long poems in languages like Greek
or French, and I do not really know these languages at
all. Naturally I cannot remember my poems next day,
and probably it is the same thing with all the speeches
and discussions of my dreams. Probably I never say
anything sensible, and anyway there is no one who
hears me.

'What was it that I have just dreamed? I dreamed that there was a huge cavern of ice, green and glittering and immensely beautiful, great sheer walls of it for miles and miles, like waves of emerald. This was of great importance, though I am not sure why. But I was in a little house lying on the floor with my baby close to me. Yet he was not a baby then; he was a little boy, old enough to clasp his hands around my neck so that I could not move when it was necessary for me to move.

'Low down on the wall facing me there was a kind of hole with a hinged wooden covering. It seemed the only exit from the room, and I knew that I must reach it. But there was a weight over my legs and the little boy kept his arms tight about my neck so that I could only struggle forward gradually. Then I heard the tremendous roar and splintering and crash of the ice, and I knew that there were great walls and cliffs of it somewhere outside this house. I began to feel sick and I saw the structure of the house bend and the door towards which I was just extending my hand begin to crumple so that its covering was jammed and so that anyway the aperture would be too small to allow us through it. I said to myself "This is an earthquake," and all around me was still the clash and groaning of the ice.

'What could this dream have meant? I must try to remember it. Perhaps it was something to do with an air raid. Or was it that my boy is in some danger and I might have saved him? Or is it that I think that the whole world is breaking up and there will never be any more happiness for anyone?

'But there *were* happy times. When I was engaged. At the dance, when we went outside and I was trembling

with love and fear so that I could not speak. The moon
was like a servant to us, drenching our paths with light,
and the black trees all around seemed friendly too.
When he began to speak he also was trembling. And
when we came back and all the faces looked different
and unreal though they were looking at us kindly
enough. Then when we were standing by the river and
saw a bird, it must have been a kingfisher, flashing away
from us. If anyone else had seen us there he would have
thought we were mad, we were so happy.

'And then suddenly in that same night that we saw
the kingfisher everything changed. I should have known
before but I could not believe it. He was bound to go.
Was he cruel to do so? No. His death was part of him.
I should not have argued with him, since it was no good.
But why do men run the world so badly? So badly that
all the best of them are dragged into the mistakes of all
the worst. It would be better if they left it to women,
who would think more of men than they do of themselves or of women either.

'Oh, even after that there were happy times, even
though I thought they would never return. There were
Dick's schooldays and the picnics we had, going in the
dogcart. There was his stamp collection and the time
when he caught a rare butterfly. When he first learned
to swim, and when he thought I was going to marry
Mr. Millington. How we laughed at that! Mr. Millington would have been offended if he had heard what we
said about him. There were the evenings we used to
have with Uncle Tom when Dick would read aloud to
us and everyone would say how intelligent he was, everyone except me, for fear of spoiling him, though I lis-

tened to his praises more eagerly than he did himself.

'And there were strange times too. When he was confirmed and I thought that he was taking it all too seriously; for he would ask odd questions. Once he said "Is it right for me to have two overcoats when some people haven't any?" I told him that we were poor enough, which was true, but he still was not satisfied. About this time I came across a notebook which he kept. On one page he had written in illuminated letters "God is Love" and after that "Peace and Joy for ever. Everything that lives is holy." I think that that is a quotation from a book, but I cried when I read it, since it reminded me of what I felt when I was young, what I still feel, only that I know that it is no good feeling like this in this world.

'Perhaps I was wrong to read his private notebook without his permission, but it charmed me to see the way he wrote. It was sententious and foolish as such writings usually are, but it showed his good heart. On one page he had written "No war can be justified" and he had underlined this carefully in red ink. When I read it I was filled with horror, for I imagined suddenly that it was possible that there would be another war. That was like a nightmare which I have just had. It was something about some ice. But now it does not seem to me so terrifying as it did.'

Here she opened her eyes for a moment and looked directly at the place where I was standing. Then she turned her head aside so that she seemed to be scrutinizing the two photographs on the bed table. She sighed and again her eyes closed. I noticed that now she was sleeping more peacefully, and I listened to the words which I heard or seemed to hear on her lips.

'Why was it that after this the really happy times became fewer and there was more and more of perplexity and sorrow? I was sorry when he lost interest in religion, for it made him sometimes talk cynically. I was worried when he began to fall in love with girls. It was not because I was jealous. It was because neither he nor they seemed to expect or want the kind of happiness which I had sought and found. His young friends seemed to me feverish and materialistic and cynical. But he was always kind to me.

' "They tell us," he said once, "that we are living in an age of transition. It feels more like living on a volcano."

'And of course he was right, though I did not believe it at the time. He smiled when he said this, but I knew that he was not joking. He said that when he was married he might be able to see into the future, but as it was he could see nothing there, or nothing that made sense. But he did not want to get married. He had views about sex which at first rather shocked me, though I loved him for having the confidence to tell me what he thought. He behaved very badly, I am afraid, to that girl whom he once brought to see me; but I expect it was as much her fault as his. And in the end he was right. What he really wanted was a wife whom he could love.

'But it seems that nowadays the young people are so suspicious of each other that they are afraid to love properly. It seems that they fear the past and that they fear the future. What was that he said—that he could not see into the future? That was why he used to dislike his job, though it was quite a good job, and why he sometimes drank too much when he couldn't afford it. I think that he is right. When he gets married he will see the future as I have seen it. He will choose a good wife. He's sensible enough now. And I shall be able to help them in all kinds of ways.

'But when was it that he said "I cannot see into the future"? What was that dream I had? It was something about a door which I could not reach.'

Again she turned over on her back and I saw her move her head restlessly from side to side. She was frowning, and her lips moved uneasily as her sleep became less tranquil. She did not open her eyes, and I continued to listen to what she said or thought.

'It was in that big beechwood,' she said, 'at the beginning of spring. It was like walking under the sea in that green light with the sun just twinkling above us and our feet gently sinking into the softened ground. And as I talked it seemed to me that I was in another time and place, so that all I said and all I felt was hopeless and already destined. And yet I spoke urgently. I tried to shake myself free of the clogging and numbing feeling that this was a conversation which had already taken place. Perhaps it was because he listened politely, just as his father had done, that I knew how objectless my words were.

'Yet there was a difference too. It was a great difference. My husband was sure that he was right. He thought that he could see the future clear, although really what he saw was illusion; but Dick was not sure at all. Only

he too was equally determined to go. He agreed with
my arguments and then he shrugged his shoulders. "I
know it doesn't make sense," he said, and then he added
"but does peace make sense either?"

'I accused him of being thoughtless and unimagina-
tive, though I knew that he was neither. I asked him
how he could face the fact of killing or maiming a
fellow man, of dropping bombs on people who shivered
and cowered below, old people and children. And again
he said "What happens in peace? Minds and bodies are
still killed, though more slowly. All you object to is the
direct action of pressing a button or a lever. To me it is
horrible too, but cleaner than the hypocrisies of peace."

'And all the time the green light streamed down upon
us and the birds were singing.

'"I may be wrong," he said, "but it seems better to
get something done, to achieve some kind of result,
than to go on living as we have done, aimlessly, irre-
sponsibly. It is a kind of disease that has to work itself
out. One can't stand aside from it. I know that I have
my part to play in it."

'Then he was speaking very seriously and I knew that
my words were useless. It was then that he said "I cannot see the future," and he smiled slowly. He used to
smile like that when he was a child and on his way to
bed. But now there was something sadder and more
desperate about that smile than anything which I had
seen before. How the young must hate and despise the
old for the world in which they find themselves! Even
when he was a baby I used to think of him as grown-up,
though it was funny and impossible to do so. I always

thought of him as happy and energetic and full of life.
I never saw that sad smile. What I thought of was him
only and not the world in which he would live.

'He never blamed me. He never blamed anyone,
unless you could call that smile an expression of blame,
and those words, "I cannot see the future."

'I was dreaming of some ice, miles and miles of it,
beautifully green like that light which came to us
through the young beech leaves; and the ice was splintering and shaking all around. It was dangerous and I
was trapped somewhere. It was like a picture that I saw
in the paper.

'I say that I cannot bear to read the papers nowadays,
and yet I often do read them. But how I hate their cruel
headlines and their smug articles, all the big words
which are day by day persuading people that war is not
a crime. They are like fetters on people's minds and
people are so loaded with them that they cannot move
towards the good and simple things which the heart sees.
Instead they drag themselves clumsily among the big
words and forget their own hearts.

'The picture I saw was of some bombed homes. In
one of them a baby had just been born, and the mother
and child had been saved. They do not take pictures of
the babies who are not saved.

'Oh God save him! God help him! Let him be happy
after the war! Let it not be selfish of me to pray like
this. He is all that I have. He did not want to do anyone
any harm.'

Her lips ceased to move. She sighed deeply and seemed
to relax in a more genuine sleep. I could see the faint
trace of tears on her closed eyelashes and remembered

how I had seen them before on her younger face and how the baby whom then she was holding in her arms had looked wonderingly upon them.

Either now, or soon, I knew that he would be falling from the sky, dead already by cannon fire or to die on impact with the ground.

Again his mother would receive visits from friends who would attempt to console her for her loss, but she would think chiefly of her son who had lost everything and in particular that encouraging future which she had dreamed, prayed or imagined both for him and for herself.

CHAPTER VIII

The Priest

1

STILL, for a moment or two, I looked upon the sleeping face, although even now I seemed to know that soon I should have seen the last of it. And as I looked I was filled once more with a feeling that was both sweet and bitter, a deep sympathy for all those women who had suffered as had this one, whether their intellectual convictions had been the same or different. I began to see now that children, lovers and mothers were often so gifted as to be able to see something very like the vision which I had seen at the time of my death, only with this difference, that for them the exciting prospect of the world seemed naturally inviting and certainly accessible, whereas I had discovered, at the same moment with its intricacy and grandeur, its remoteness from me and inaccessibility.

It was true that the actions and events of the future were, as I had seen, cruelly at variance with their brilliant expectations, yet what they had expected was real too, as I had the best of reasons for believing, nor could I look with equal sympathy upon those others

who, like Sir Alfred Fothey or Bob Clark, appeared to
regard themselves as established in a state of affairs
so crushing and so cruel to generosity, enterprise and
tenderness.

This woman in front of me, hoping against hope in
her sleep for the safety of her son, seemed to me to
possess a fuller knowledge of what I understood to be
the value of life than had any of the others.

The others, no doubt, when the war was over, would
welcome every slogan for the organization of permanent peace; but for some of them this organization
would be attractive because of the prospect of uninter-
rupted commerce; others would look simply for a rest;
others would demand a roughly equal distribution of
purchasing power; and if no further aims than these
were envisaged the peace would be, I thought, unstable
and ignoble.

It was not that I agreed with the woman's outright
pacifism. Indeed I had been too deeply implicated in
war to be able to do this. It was perhaps true, I thought,
as the soldier from Spain had said, that with more able
statesmanship the war could have been avoided. But I
had been no statesman myself. For me the war had been
an atmosphere; a fact in which I was forced to live,
whether I liked it or not; nor had I had any wish to
stand aside from it until now when I was inexorably
separated from the living. Moreover, I could not help
remembering the many whom I had known whose
countries had been ravaged by the enemy. Many of them
would fight with the greater courage and resolution
because in their mind's eye was always some familiar
landscape, an orchard or stretch of open ground, or, it

might be, a scene like that one by the river where I had
watched this woman and her husband.

Memories of such dear places and of the people who
had lived in them would animate men to undergo all
kinds of hardships, and sometimes to fight with an extreme and unnecessary ferocity, avenging their losses on
others who could not reasonably be held responsible
for them, since it is impossible in the heat of battle to
pick out a villain from a hero. Yet the intense love for
one's native earth is good, nor could I feel anything but
admiration for those who fought desperately for small
patches of ground or for the memory of such patches.
Our enemies also, I knew, would be animated often by
the same sentiments, but this did not make either our
feelings or theirs any the less proper.

I began to find now that I was in a greater state of
confusion and perplexity as a result of my enquiry than
I had been when I first entered upon it. There were
indeed many others, apart from this casual group of
sightseers, whose opinion on my own predicament I
might have asked; yet I could remember from my living
experience that of these there were many who, like Sir
Alfred, were, although with a remarkable conception of
duty, almost totally blind. They were unable at all
clearly to envisage the state of mind of one like me, let
alone the millions of others, who had lost in an instant
the whole future with its hope, and who was uncertain
still as to why exactly this thing had happened; nor were
they really aware of much else that I had seen, the
herds of terrified and starving civilians huddled on the
bombed roads, ignorant of what was happening and
what would happen next, dirt and disease, the collapse

of nerves, the lust, brutality and madness which will break out from time to time in strange places, the over-whelming monotony and frightening suspicion that all our activity was meaningless.

Instead of appreciating these things, such people would consider only our acts of daring and of comrade-ship which, though true and splendid enough, consti-tuted only a part of the story. After the war was over they would be pleased by what they would call "Victory" and a return to the old ways. They would remember with pride their own sacrifices, whatever these had been, and for us, no doubt, they would erect another monu-ment. They would speak highly of us at all times, but would hardly imagine what men we were or what lives we might have led. It would not often occur to them that they were in any sense responsible for our deaths.

There were many too who, like Bob Clark, had at an early age so constricted their vision as to ensure them-selves against disappointment. Such people would be proud to call themselves "realists," having no use for such conceptions as "glory" and "honour" which, in their view, belonged only to the past. They would be content if they could keep their jobs, with salaries regu-larly rising, if they could be immune from the most obvious dangers, if their wives could be presentable, if they could enjoy at a reasonable price those entertain-ments which from time to time were most fashionable. There were many like this, and they would be wholly uninterested in any question which I might care to put to them.

Unlike Sir Alfred they would not even pretend to honour our memory, though they might sometimes speak of us in conventionally reverent tones. They would regard us as much less fortunate than themselves and not only that, but, in a way, inferior, rather as though we were fellow-workers who, owing to a lack of skill or of influence, were receiving lower salaries than the average. We would be, in their view, people who had been caught up into a dangerous affair which was neither ours nor theirs. Some accident of age or some acquired ability might, they would think, have preserved us in a normal way of life. As it was we were to be pitied, but not much remembered.

So much, I thought, for Sir Alfred Fothey and for Bob Clark. Both had voiced feelings that, at one time or another, had been mine; yet these feelings now had no kind of relevance to the situation in which I stood. Both, it now seemed to me, were content with horizons of sympathy and ambition so narrow as to constitute an almost meaningless view. I could not pretend to any exhilaration at the thought that my death might have made such views more generally popular or more stable.

With the others into whose lives I had entered for a moment or two I felt greater sympathy, even although they also had failed to provide a satisfactory answer to my question. There was some comfort in the thought that my death may have helped in the destruction of that monstrous barbarity from which the old refugee, his son and so many others, had suffered; yet this thought, in itself, could not wholly satisfy me. I was bound to remember that this barbarism was no isolated phenomenon. It was part of a scheme of life which, in its whole, was capable of being represented as noble, or at least more noble than were the views of Sir Alfred, of Bob Clark and of others like them.

Indeed it was, I thought, to some extent a reaction from those views, and, if those views had not prevailed, then this savagery would not have been able to arise. To have helped to liberate men and women from the effects of savagery was indeed, if I had really done so, a worthy achievement; yet even this seemed to me hardly sufficient to justify the death and destruction of so much. If the roots and conditions for savagery remained the expenditure would be out of all proportion to the result achieved.

Indeed, as the soldier from Spain had reminded me, no one race or nation enjoyed a monopoly in barbarism and in cruelty. The most monstrous inhumanity and injustice has proceeded as often from mere callousness as from a misdirected sense of duty; and this callousness, just as the more evident brutality, was as often as not the result of fear. Certainly I was impelled to sympathize with this soldier, for he and the woman, whom I still saw sleeping in the bed, alone of all whom I had examined, seemed to have imagined a life which was, to my present view, at all worth living. He had thought of freedom as of something which could not exist in isolation from others and he had claimed that the freedom which he wished to promote was as extensive as the world.

It was a noble purpose, and had I been able to believe that my own activities had been deliberately designed to further such a purpose, I should have been proud indeed. But the memory of Sir Alfred, of Bob Clark, of the experience of this soldier himself and of my own experiences was still too vivid for me to believe that so far-reaching an ideal had really animated those in whose names we had gone out to fight. Moreover, when I compared this idea itself with the vision which I myself had seen, there seemed to me something in it which was both rigid and incomplete. There was a harshness, almost a desperation, in many of the phrases which the soldier from Spain had used. This was understandable enough, so frustrated had been his generous feelings and most devoted plans. It was natural for him to insist first of all on justice, on rectitude, and to postpone to the future those other qualities of living which were, to my mind, at least equally valuable. But still, this simplification was a source of incompleteness. It was true, as the woman had said, that his ideals could be as cruel as could any others.

There was, I thought, when I reflected upon what I had seen myself, a warmth and beauty and fascination in life which are not associated with the idea of plain rectitude; and an appreciation of these qualities is necessary if we are to hold our heads up and face that underlying horror and insecurity of which the friend of the soldier from Spain had spoken with such evident conviction. What he had said was too true. Had I not seen it myself when I had seen the rest, my body lying to disintegrate on the smoky and pulsating ground?

Indeed this soldier from Spain, so far from helping me, had served only to confuse me further. Far more deliberately than I had done he had fought for a world in which he believed. It was a better world than that which existed but it was not the world which I had seen. All his efforts had been cruelly frustrated and his continued confidence might seem to many rather the result of a determined courage than of common sense or a feeling for evidence. What wonder if he became as merciless to others as others had been to him and to his friends? Might it be, I wondered, that this way alone there was any hope? Yet the thought appalled me. My interest was with the life I might have led and with the lives of those now living. I could not but regard with repugnance the thought of further bloodshed for our children and perhaps for theirs, till in a remote future justice was forcibly established.

Still more was I confused when I thought of the woman who lay on the bed in front of me, now sleeping in apparent peace. I shared with her the view which she had had of the beauty and exhilaration of life. Yet this vision had been the occasion to her of more unhappiness than of happiness. It had cut her off from the community in which she lived, so that she was unable confidently to express either her joy or her sorrow. Those whom she loved had not reached the same conclusions as she had done, so that in a sense she had been cut off from them too. Thus the world which she saw as beautiful and forgiving had taken forcibly from her just the things which she most valued, and left her no substance, only the memory of certain moments and of an incomplete devotion.

It began to appear to me that those who valued life most were most inevitably disappointed, and, if this were true, I thought, why should anyone choose to live rather than to die? Were these wars, in which this woman's husband and son and I myself had lost life, gigantic attempts at liberation by suicide from insupportable conditions? The thought was horrible. I closed my eyes and, when I opened them, found myself again in the religious building.

2

My eyes no longer rested upon the face of the woman whom I had just seen in sleep. I saw the whole scene together in front of me, and it may have been that, in my abstraction, I had allowed some words to pass unnoticed; for now it appeared that the sightseers were preparing to leave the chapel where I stood. They were looking at each other as people do who have agreed to differ, though without much ill-feeling. No doubt each of them had often previously in the past spoken the same words or words like those which I had heard from them, and now some of them seemed in a way abashed as though, considering the sacred character of the building, they had expressed themselves too freely.

Some were looking intently at me, though without seeing me; others reflectively allowed their eyes to rest upon the grey and drooping flags, records of so many centuries of warfare, and upon the high vaulted roof with its religious emblems.

The priest stood somewhat apart from the rest, with his hands folded in front of him. He was staring at the floor almost at the point where my foot rested on the stone, and he did not raise his head as the sightseers' guide tapped vigorously with his stick upon the ground, wishing evidently to attract the attention of his party to some other quarter of the building. Indeed the face of this black-robed official expressed both impatience and indignation, for he had no doubt been compelled, owing to the intervention of the priest, to stay much longer than usual in one spot, and to listen to a conversation which to his mind had clearly been unnecessary and incorrect. Now he cleared his throat and pronounced the words:

'In an adjoining chapel we have some remarkable records of the military history of the medieval times.'

The group followed him. Some bowed to the priest, but he did not appear to notice them, and they went away out of sight, their footsteps ringing together on the stones. I followed them closely with my eyes, reflecting to myself that I knew them much better than any of them would expect, and that I was unlikely ever to see them again. As their bodies and their shadows merged in with the shadows of the huge pillars of the nave, or passed out of sight behind projections of the towering stone, they appeared to me as almost insubstantial things, figures of a dream, drifting to and fro on no evident course in an environment which was too vast for them to be significant within it. And as the feeble sound of their footsteps died away I began to think of them with a strange affection and fellow-feeling, bearing them no resentment for their inability to explain my own perplexity.

Indeed how could I have hoped that they would ever be able to do so? Had I not myself in the past, at various times, thought as each of these people thought, and why should I imagine that now they would be wiser than I was? If ignorance was pitiable then both they and I were to be pitied. And if I was perhaps more conscious of my ignorance than they were, that was the accident of my situation rather than any merit which would entitle me to feel superior to them.

There had been, I knew, philosophers who had looked on the world of men much as I was doing now, from an unusual angle, divorced from the uneasy passions, fears, ambitions and enthusiasm in which the majority of people live. To many of these great thinkers the hurry and bustle, stress and storm of ordinary life has seemed a mere illusion, evil or meaningless, when compared with the great truths which the contemplative could grasp and enjoy within his own mind.

To me also, as I watched the departing sightseers, all their agitation and emphasis seemed somehow pathetic, and themselves, as I have said, not greatly significant among these historic walls and in the growing darkness of the air. Yet I lacked wholly that philosophic calm with which such a view of things might have been calculated to inspire me. In my situation, and with the memory of what I had seen on the battlefield still fresh in my mind, I could not but differ from some of these great philosophers in attaching to the actuality of life a value which to them, no doubt, would seem extravagant.

For it was just this that most of all I desired to find— a significance in the living. If I could find it, then it seemed to me that my own death would be capable of explanation.

This conviction of mine may appear strange to others, but I felt it intensely. It was not so much that I wished to be assured that the war in which I had lost my life would result in a state of affairs in which peace would be permanent, though that in itself, I knew, would be a worthy achievement. But I wanted more than this. I

wanted the belief that peace was what the living desired.
I wanted to be freed from the uneasy suspicion that
many in their heart of hearts had not found, or would
not find, life worth living.

My mind reverted to the first few minutes of time
during which I had found myself in this abbey or
cathedral. The priest had been praying indiscriminately
for all, friend or foe alike, who had lost their lives as I
had done, and when I had asked him whether this
gigantic slaughter had been the will of God, he had
replied that it was the result of the will of man. This,
at the beginning of my enquiry, I had been inclined
to doubt, since I knew from my own experience that
there were very few indeed who deliberately enjoyed
warfare. But now I began to revise my opinion.

If men's wills, I thought, were set in a certain direction war might well be the inevitable result, even
though no one had clearly envisaged it as such. And
when I remembered what I had seen of the sightseers,
the total frustration of the best of them, the indifference
and stupidity of the worst, the insignificance and in-
effectiveness of them all, it began to seem to me that I
had been the spectator of merely mechanical and pre-
ordained activities, of people so caught up and impris-
oned in the blind vehicle of history that all their actions
and aspirations had no more meaning than a collection
of flies buzzing together in a glass bottle. Even those who
fancied that they had a clear idea of where they wanted
to go found this direction barred to them by the activities of others. Even those who had actually seen the
enchanting possibilities of existence were immediately
swept away, as by a general tide from the shores which

they had glimpsed. There was a set of the will against the beauty and the excitement and the tranquillity which I had seen too late.

The will of man, it seemed, was not to be liberated, not to adventure, not to live. And so man's will worked itself out in the violent deaths of millions. Could one give the name of "will" to so blind a manifestation? Or could one call this trap in which humanity seemed fixed to jostle aimlessly "the will of God"?

I had reached this point in my reflections when I looked up and saw that the priest was watching me. I looked too at the great cross on the altar behind him, the lines of drooping flags, the massive pillars, and, in my present mood, the whole structure seemed to me more like a vast and constricting mausoleum than a place of worship. The walls were full of history, but the record, I thought, was more of centuries of bloodshed than of heroism.

The priest spoke to me and said, 'I did not notice that you had returned. Did you listen to the conversation?'

I nodded my head and it was no doubt clear to him that what I had seen and heard had given me little satisfaction.

'When you think,' he said, 'of the long history of man on earth——'

But here I interrupted him. 'I was thinking of that,' I said, 'and also of the short period of time which belongs to any one man here.'

The priest raised his head and looked at me keenly. 'So was I,' he said. 'Indeed when one thinks at all it seems that one is driven to think in terms that are in a way contradictory.'

I nodded my head in agreement, for he had expressed what I felt myself. The whole of my dilemma had originated from that first simultaneous vision of beauty and destruction, life and death.

The priest continued:

'Why is it that at all times living men, whose lives have been so short and insecure, so vexed by poverty and war, ignorance, perplexity and deceit, who have as a rule failed to understand each other or the world in which they live, whose actions may well seem for the most part rather clumsy and disgraceful than very glorious—why is it that they have spent much of their little time and energy in recording their exploits, in building monuments like the one in which we stand, in the choice and preservation of flags, tombs and symbols?'

He paused and I shrugged my shoulders, for at the moment I could not think of a fitting answer. Finally, since he continued to gaze at me inquisitively, I said:

'Perhaps it is because they realize their insignificance, and they try, by identifying themselves with some group or other, to make themselves seem more important and their lives more worth while. Is it not a vast deception?'

The priest kept his eyes fixed on mine. He seemed to be full of pity for me and I was at a loss to account for this attitude, since he could not possibly have any idea of my real predicament. His look was like that of one who waits patiently for a pupil to remember some obvious point which the pupil himself has unaccountably forgotten. But I had no more to say and the priest spoke again.

'Surely,' he said, and as he spoke he turned his head so that he could see the large cross above the altar, 'we believe that there can be nothing so significant and so important as man—unless we are thinking of God.'

His remark surprised me, although indeed what I had seen at the moment of my death had already suggested to me that what he said was true. Yet to believe in the significance of man was one thing, to find evidence for one's belief another.

'So you do not believe,' I said, 'in this forming of men into groups and this artificial self-aggrandizement?'

He smiled before he said, 'How can one not believe in what one sees every day and what one sees often to be so good? I fear we are misunderstanding each other. I mentioned these memorials which men have made of their collaboration as good things, not as anything either deceptive or pathetic. There have been tribes and clans, there have been regiments, armies, clubs; there have been countries and even empires of which the members have shared to a certain extent in a fellow feeling of self-respect and self-sacrifice. Members of these associations have known that, within greater or less limits, they can depend on each other for support and sympathy and understanding. They have shared together what they believed to be their triumphs and their disasters. Is not this an admirable thing? Has it not heightened the life and the imagination of each individual? Has it not deserved a memorial?'

I felt some disappointment at hearing him speak in this way. Not that what he said was untrue, but he appeared to me only to be voicing rather more emphatically the views which I had heard expressed by Sir Alfred Fothey, and to be indifferent to my own position which was of one who, together with millions, had

suffered from the interaction of these groups which
filled him with such admiration.

'As often as not,' I said, 'memorials and celebrations
are devoted to the number of men who have been
killed.'

He glanced at me quickly and I noticed again a
strange sympathy in his eye. 'Just now,' he said, 'we de-
cided that our thought was usually involved in a consideration of opposites. Nothing that is partial can be
completely good, or, for that matter, completely bad.
And men have realized this. That is why their associations have grown bigger and bigger.'

'And more and more destructive,' I added, but the
priest, though by a quick movement of the head he
showed that he had heard my remark, was pursuing his
own train of thought. He turned his eyes round upon
the religious building where we stood and said:

'There is another point. Have you observed how frequently these organizations of men are associated with
the idea of God? That may seem to you a small thing.
To me it is naturally of the first importance. It seems to
me to show that men do recognize, however dimly, the
inadequacy and danger even of their own forms of
brotherhood. They realize the weakness of their own
wills and imaginations, and they band themselves together in confederations which for a certain time and
for certain purposes give them strength and confidence
in one another. Then they begin to realize the inadequacy of these federations, and they grope towards a
greater strength and a greater communion that may be
attained at some future date. What ought to be the evo-
lution of these groups of which we are speaking? They

ought to grow bigger and bigger, from family to town, from town to nation, from nation to confederation, from confederation to world. And if man's mind could keep pace with the growing breadth and complexity of organization, his mind too would grow capable of a sense of brotherhood far richer than anything which he has known, indeed of a wholly different quality.

'But, as you rightly point out, this has not happened. Man's ability to form associations has reached a certain point and then stopped. And at this point, as though to remind him of the difficult further step from which he shrinks, death and destruction on an unprecedented scale have intervened. Why can he not take this further step? There are many reasons, and they are closely associated together. For one thing his imagination is weak and undeveloped. He will behave with extraordinary self-sacrifice towards those who march with him under the same flag, because he has shared their life and their dangers and his fellowship with them has given a fragmentary but none the less real access of meaning to his own existence. He cannot often see himself as a fellow man with his enemies who are undergoing precisely the same dangers as himself; still less can he think of himself as a partner and collaborator with those of completely different races and customs who perhaps have not yet developed to his present and dangerous state of organization. Yet he must take this further step in fellowship if he is to survive.

'There are other difficulties too. Some appear to be merely practical, such as the sensible organization of the world's economic resources. You might think that every sane person would wish to see this done so as to

secure the maximum benefit to everyone. Unfortunately
this is not what most people desire. Inside the national
organizations there exist other groups of great complexity and prestige, groups of the privileged and the
unprivileged, rich and poor, skilled and semi-skilled,
and these groups will fight against each other with perhaps greater fury than do the national groups in an
international war. You must have observed the paradox
that the·nation itself reaches a greater degree of unity
when it is organized to kill than when it is organized for
a life of peace. And so the problem of using the wealth
of the world for living men is by no means entirely
practical. It cannot be solved on any other assumption
except that each man's life is equally valuable and
equally to be respected. Men have not yet, except in a
few cases, made this assumption. But if they do not make
it they will perish.

'There is only one authority for the making of this
assumption and for that other belief too, the brotherhood of man. It is the belief in God. It was because of
a dim recognition of this fact that men first began to
associate their groups with the name of God. In so
doing they emphasize not only the value of their groups
but also their essential unimportance and partiality.
When they cease to submit their confederations to a
greater and in many ways a dimmer idea, they will worship their confederations for their own sake, and they
themselves will become inhuman. Perhaps you find this
conclusion unlikely or unfamiliar to you.'

He stopped speaking and looked at me, waiting for
a reply. I had followed his words with attention, partly
for their own sake and partly because they reminded me

strangely of what had been said earlier by the soldier from Spain, although certainly the conclusion reached by the priest was a different one. It was indeed a conclusion which did not strike me as self-evident. I waited for a few moments before replying and then said:

'Perhaps I have not yet grasped your meaning. What I have noticed is that in war the priests of religion on both sides bless the armies and persuade the soldiers of the justice of their cause. There appears to be some inconsistency in this attitude. I have been informed myself that I was fighting against the enemies of God, and so, I have no doubt, was the enemy.'

Here the priest looked grave and then, to my surprise, he burst into a laugh.

'How can man be an enemy of God?' he said. 'It was pompous and inaccurate language which they used to you. But is it sensible to lose your belief in God simply because you have heard priests employ language that is inconsistent with their religion? Do you expect priests to be immune from the failings of other men? As for blessing armies, why not? Does God cease to be interested in a man when he has become a soldier? It may be that it is more necessary for the soldier than for any other man to be reminded of God and to seek his blessing. For the soldier is in more danger than are most people of losing that most priceless of possessions, the consciousness of his own soul, and of the vastness of its prospects.

'You know what an army is, the closest and in some ways the most mechanical of confederations. Weeks of training are devoted to what seem the simplest tasks, so that each man can respond automatically to the needs

of the group of which he is a part. There is an immense
elaboration of responsibility. One man's action may be
vital to the success of a whole campaign and yet the man
himself may know nothing of this since he has no idea of
the purpose of what he is doing. Yet in a good army the
soldier is no automaton. He must be capable himself of
making decisions, and there are times when his private
initiative may influence the view of the commander-in-
chief. It is a remarkably integrated world in which he
lives, a world which can breed the finest qualities, and
yet its purpose is, as you pointed out, something that in
itself is clearly evil, the destruction of life.

'There are other contradictions also. In the very perfection of this organization which has finally so evil an
aim is the danger that the soldier may forget that the
aim is evil and that the integration, for all its perfection,
is partial. He may regard the group as finally more important than the individual because incidentally and
for certain purposes it really appears to be so. Indeed
without faith in something bigger than the group of
which he is a part I do not see how he can avoid this
danger. Some are able to envisage the world as a greater
unity than their national army, but there are very few
who can do this without a belief in God. Indeed without
a belief in God a belief in the world seems scarcely
logical.'

He stopped speaking and I saw, when I looked at him,
that his face was tired and almost discontented, as though
he were profoundly dissatisfied with what he had said.
For my part I regarded his words as inconclusive, and
yet, it had affected me to find that he was so deeply
conscious of those very contradictions which had never

ceased to perplex me. But his solution of them, if indeed he imagined that he had found one, was to me, at this stage, inadequate and incomprehensible.

'I do not understand you,' I said. 'At one moment you appear to admire vast organizations of men, such as armies are, and at the next moment you agree that their purpose is evil and you admire only the individual soul. For this attitude of mind I have a fellow-feeling, for in a way it is my own. But still the attitude is self-contradictory. It leads only to perplexity and, if it is more true than most, it is also more uncomfortable.'

I spoke somewhat indignantly, and he looked hard at me, as though surprised at my indignation, before he replied.

'It is certainly difficult for us,' he said, 'using the words which we do use, to understand each other. Nevertheless let us continue to try. And first let me say that to recognize the complexity of things should not necessarily lead to discouragement. When, for example, we look at a landscape we observe an infinite variety of colours and shapes. Our senses of hearing, smell and touch may also be occupied at the same time. Yet the variety and complexity of the whole fill us with delight. Why is this? Because we recognize it as a whole, even though we are unacquainted with many of the details which compose it. If we lacked this recognition how terrifying and confusing would the prospect seem! In the mere juxtaposition of a sheep, say, and a tree there would be something madly incongruous if we were unaware of the earth which supports them both and of the sky above them. Both our perception and our knowledge are gradual and grow only by the recognition of the connection between things and at the same time of each thing's uniqueness.

'I need not, I think, tell you how bewildering and exciting is the whole of life; but it is too bewildering and too exciting altogether unless men have some conception of its wholeness and of its purpose. People cannot live without some conception of this kind and some have found it at a very low level. If, for instance, we could really get to know those few sightseers who were here just now we should find an extraordinary variety among them. For some the world would be bounded only by their own interests; and do not think that here I am wholly condemning them. Our smallest actions have illimitable effects and our simplest assumptions have aspects that turn in every direction. There is a great difference between one whose self-interest is entirely conventional, who looks no farther than his particular comfort and prestige, and the self-interest of another who is occupied entirely with his love for a fellow-human being and who, through his love, is perhaps able to view the whole world as though it were made beautiful for this occupation. The first of these people will, in many ways, be able to live more harmoniously with his fellows than the second; but it is the attitude of the second which I think that you and I are more inclined to respect, because it seems to us to be, however wrong, yet nearer to the truth of things.

'But no concentration of the mind can isolate us from the effects of our real relationship with an infinite number of other people, alive, dead and to be born. Nor is one any more secure or necessarily more admirable if one's self-interest is identified with that of a nation or a

class. These very pre-occupations will lead to injustice
and lack of sympathy towards individuals both classified
and unclassified.'

Here I interrupted him to protest. 'That is just what
I was saying. All these views are partial, all contain some
truth, all are disappointing. Men wander to and fro,
half-blind, killing each other for various motives and
being killed. Where is the comfort in this? Even if you
know the beauty and the extent of life where is the
comfort? There is less of it then.'

'Less comfort,' said the priest, 'if one believes in God
than if one does not? I see that you are serious, but I cannot think that you are right. No, there is comfort simply
in this fact, that we can perceive our limitations and
measure them against our desires. There is comfort in
the fact that we need comfort. Otherwise we should
really be blind. Think of those sightseers who have just
left and of the question which we put to them. Each of
them gave a different answer, and each answer was to
some extent true. You were dissatisfied however with
their answers because all of them together seemed to you
incommensurable with the urgency of the question and
with the fact of the destruction of life which you had in
mind. How much more dissatisfied would you have been
If they had all agreed upon one of the answers which they
gave? And if you can imagine yourself as having in your
turn agreed with them would you choose to have done
so and to have been content?

'Perhaps you would like me to attempt to answer your
question. But I know that my answer would be, in its
way, as limited as were the answers of the others. I can
only say that not the simplest question can be fully

answered without referring it to the whole visible and
invisible world; and this none of us can do. It is impossible for us, with our limited understanding, to
justify any evil; and the evils, both of peace and war,
are many. We can trace, no doubt, in politics and in
economics and in sociology, many of the evils which
cause war, and to trace them and cure them is of the
utmost importance. But this we can only do with a
horizon before our eyes much vaster than men have had
hitherto and (though in a sense, it is the same thing)
with an attention to detail much more accurate and
loving than has been known previously.

'If all men could see themselves as this unknown
soldier of whom we were speaking, and who has been
killed, if they could be aware of the perplexity which
he would naturally feel, then they might become conscious of his need and of what I believe to be the will
of God. They would know the comradeship which war
and danger can develop, and they would know the in-
sufficiency of that comradeship unless it is extended
farther and farther. They would know how for certain
purposes the individual must subordinate himself to
the group, and how finally it is the individual who is
uniquely capable of life and death. They might come
to realize, just through this destruction, the immense
value and distinction of life. If they came to do so there
would be at least a certain sense in which it would be
true to say that so much death was worth while.'

He paused for a moment before speaking again, and
I saw that his eyes were half closed as if he were endeavouring to summon up some picture before his mind.

'I am thinking,' he said, 'of the enormous goodness

and beauty and fascination of life, all the sights and sounds and colours, tastes in the mouth, textures of things touched, the warmth and tenderness of love, the delight in the mind's insight and exploration, the sweetness of some moods, a million things which you will readily imagine. And side by side with this I envisage the most elaborate apparatus for destruction, twisted metal, broken bodies, a whole curriculum of slaughter in which men and women are trained from their early youth.'

He looked at me now very sharply and then continued, again with his eyes half-closed.

'I imagine,' he said, 'that any soldier, and perhaps the one of whom we were speaking, may have thought as I am now thinking, either dying or before death. He might see with a peculiar intensity either what I have attempted to describe or something like it. Perhaps he might represent this vision to himself by symbols. He might, for example, remember some particular mountain valley and find, for some reason, in that memory a means for considering the whole depth and importance of life. And contrasted with it he might see or imagine that he sees his own distorted body and the bodies of others thrown away on the ground.

'Would not such a sight, seen, as I imagine it, clearly and distinctly, be unusually moving to him? Yet it would be strangely discouraging also if he thought that it was a sight visible to him alone. If he thought so, he might well despair and consider that both his life and his death were meaningless, and the whole world of men a procession of insignificant shadows. Yet in reality he should know that, though others may lack, for one reason or other, the precise clarity of his vision, what he has seen, and perhaps even more than he has seen is visible to everyone if they will open their eyes. That conviction would, I think, at least be worth something to him.'

As he spoke I felt for the first time since I had begun my enquiry a feeling of some satisfaction, and this was due not merely to the priest's words, but also to what I saw; for, as he opened his eyes, I stared into them and in their pupils saw not only my own reflection but the reflection of what I had seen simultaneously at the moment of my death, both the battlefield and that sunny valley which, as the priest had seemed to know, had symbolized to me a whole world of beauty and opportunity. But there was a difference in this sight which I saw now. For in being confronted with this vision of my own in the eyes of another the balance and, as it were, the contours of the view appeared to have altered. It was not that I did not see the lifeless legs in front of me or was unaware of the grimly distorted faces of the bodies at my side. They were real enough and still filled me with pity and with horror. Rather it was the other aspect of my double vision which had changed; for previously the two sights, in spite of the sweetness of the one, had combined to cause me perplexity and foreboding. And this, I now began to see, was because of my awareness of my isolation in a dead world, and shut out from the world of life.

But now, through the intervention of another, my isolation was ended, and this fact in itself was to me of such importance that it overrode all else. I looked with a new zest on the sweeping hillsides and the distant plains before me, heard more delightfully the rippling of the mountain stream, and stared with a fuller joy into the expanding distance which now appeared to me populated and filled not only with what I had seemed to have lost but with what others might really find. My picture was no longer one that might be painted by a contemplative or an æsthete or by the imagination of regret. It was a world which would be created or discovered as it was either gradually or suddenly perceived. And this in itself was a reflection which filled me with such exhilaration that I listened with rather less attention than before to the priest who was saying:

'That would be something at least, although it is true that the picture which we have imagined is a picture only, inaccurate in many respects, exaggerated in others.'

I stepped away from the stone on which I had been standing and we turned away from each other, he to the great altar where I had first seen him kneeling, and I to the West door of the abbey or cathedral, to the houses where men lived.

THE END